# Garden *of* Angels

You'll want to read these inspiring novels by

# Lurlene McDaniel

One Last Wish novels:
*Mourning Song* • *A Time to Die*
*Mother, Help Me Live* • *Someone Dies, Someone Lives*
*Sixteen and Dying* • *Let Him Live*
*The Legacy: Making Wishes Come True*
*Please Don't Die* • *She Died Too Young*
*All the Days of Her Life* • *A Season for Goodbye*
*Reach for Tomorrow*

The Dawn Rochelle novels:
*Six Months to Live* • *I Want to Live*
*So Much to Live For* • *No Time to Cry* • *To Live Again*

Other fiction by Lurlene McDaniel:
*A Rose for Melinda* • *Telling Christina Goodbye*
*How Do I Love Thee: Three Stories*
*Angel of Mercy* • *Angel of Hope*
*Starry, Starry Night: Three Holiday Stories*
*The Girl Death Left Behind*
*Angels Watching Over Me*
*Lifted Up by Angels*
*Until Angels Close My Eyes*
*Till Death Do Us Part*
*For Better, for Worse, Forever*
*I'll Be Seeing You*
*Saving Jessica*
*Don't Die, My Love*
*Too Young To Die*
*Goodbye Doesn't Mean Forever*
*Somewhere Between Life and Death*
*Time to Let Go*
*Now I Lay Me Down to Sleep*
*When Happily Ever After Ends*
*Baby Alicia Is Dying*

From every ending
comes a new beginning. . . .

# Lurlene McDaniel

# Garden *of* Angels

BANTAM BOOKS
NEW YORK • TORONTO • LONDON • SYDNEY • AUCKLAND

RL: 4.7, AGES 12 AND UP

GARDEN OF ANGELS

A Bantam Book/May 2003

Text copyright © 2003 by Lurlene McDaniel

ISBN 0-553-57093-5 (trade)—ISBN 0-553-13029-3 (GLB)

**Visit us on the Web! www.randomhouse.com/teens**
**Educators and librarians, for a variety of teaching tools, visit us at**
**www.randomhouse.com/teachers**

*Published simultaneously in the United States and Canada*

Bantam Books is an imprint of Random House Children's Books, a
division of Random House, Inc. BANTAM BOOKS and the rooster
colophon are registered trademarks of Random House, Inc.

PRINTED IN THE UNITED STATES OF AMERICA

10  9  8  7  6  5  4  3  2  1

*Dear Reader,*

*When we hear the word "cancer," it's a word that frightens. We know that cancer does not distinguish between rich and poor, fat and thin, good and bad people. Cancer can just appear, and the individual who becomes ill, as well as the family and friends of the patient, must cope. I have written many books about people who have become victims of cancer. You may have read some of them already.*

*This book is a departure in many ways from other books I've written. I have chosen to place the story in 1974 and '75, a time before many of you, my readers, were born. The setting is the Deep South, the place of my roots—the place so dear to my heart. Although this is fiction, I've included many actual events from those two years that helped shape and define the world we live in today.*

*During this time, our country was struggling to escape from a very unpopular war that we were fighting in Vietnam. The President of the United States, Richard Nixon, had to face the reality of his actions in connection to a number of scandals and voluntarily stepped down from his office. Gerald Ford was inaugurated as the new President. Bill Gates, who was twenty years old, had just founded Microsoft, but at that time technological resources and products were still years away from everyday items that people now use effortlessly. There was no e-mail. The Internet was seen as futuristic, as were home computers, cell phones and pagers. Most homes had a color television set but few had VCRs. Music was recorded on hard plastic records or on large eight-track tapes. CDs and DVDs were yet to come.*

*The first McDonald's "drive-thru" with its golden arches was opened. Disposable razors appeared in stores for the first time. Middle schools were gaining in popularity, but many kids still attended junior highs—seventh, eighth and ninth grades. Across the country, high school began with the tenth grade.*

*The popular TV shows were* All in the Family, Good Times, Maude *and* The Waltons. *What had previously been the most popular show,* The Brady Bunch, *went off the air in August 1974. October of '75 was the excitingly innovative premiere of* Saturday Night Live. *Rock star Bruce Springsteen was just starting out. Musical celebrities of those years were Elton John, Bob Dylan, George Harrison and Eric Clapton. The pop song "I Honestly Love You," sung by Olivia Newton-John, was named 1974's Record of the Year. The United States was changing, and social* issues were being more openly discussed and were being dealt with in society and in the courts.

In medicine, cancer research was at the fore-front, which it still is today. Although cancer was a major health concern, breast cancer was not discussed as openly in society. Most of today's network of support groups didn't exist yet. There were no Breast Cancer Awareness Week, no pink ribbons to symbolize the ongoing battle, no walkathons or general fund-raising efforts to eradicate the disease. Breast-saving surgeries were just beginning to be seen as a viable alternative to the more invasive and body-scarring radical mastectomy.

The treatment of breast cancer has changed dramatically in the years since 1974–1975. What has not changed is the emotional complexity of dealing with losing someone you love. Happily, today many women can "beat" breast cancer because of early detection and new treatments. The story you will read is about the love of a family—

*about how universal love is never set at a certain time: it is forever.*

*I hope the information in this note helps you better understand the time and the world in which this story is set. When you've finished the last page of this novel, I have added an endnote—I will tell you why I wrote this.*

*Sincerely,*

*Lurlene*

# Prologue

When I was fourteen years old, four things happened that shaped the course of my life. If you've ever felt that things were under control, in the blink of an eye, the world can change. Here's what happened to change my world:

American troops were pulled out of Saigon in South Vietnam, half a world away from the United States.

My sister, Adel, met Barry Sorenson, a soldier and a Yankee from New York City.

Jason Polwalski, a hunky seventeen-year-old, live-in-the-flesh juvenile deliquent from Chicago, came to live with his sister, our Baptist pastor's wife, in our town—Conners, Georgia.

And my mother, Joy Leigh Donaldson Quinlin, was diagnosed with a malignancy called

breast cancer that ate her up cell by cell while
we all stood around wringing our hands and praying prayers for healing that fell on God's deaf ears
and we visited doctors and hospitals, always
hoping.

All I knew in those days was that the protective walls of my childhood were crumbling. At
fourteen you can't be expected to have the
strength or the wisdom to shore them up.

I was born Darcy Rebecca Quinlin and raised
in Conners, population 2,900. The town had one
school that shepherded kids from the first through
the twelfth grade, four Baptist churches—three
for the whites and one for the blacks—plus a Ro-
man Catholic chapel, and a main street defined
on either end by traffic lights. As the locals liked
to say, "If you blink, you'll miss it." Conners was a
place I loved, with a history that stretched all the
way back to the early 1800s, when the Creek
Indians ceded portions of north Georgia to the
United States and settlers built log cabins in the
pine forest.

Our family home was built in 1860, right before the start of the Civil War, or as the elderly
ladies in Mama's garden club called it, the War of
Northern Aggression. My great-grandmother
Rebecca, whom I was named after, became a local
legend when, like the fictional Scarlett O'Hara,

she hid the family silver and shot herself a Yankee as Sherman was burning his way through Georgia. That happened in late 1864. The war ended seven months later.

We had farmland before the war, but most of it was sold off afterward to keep life and limb together. The house and a generous yard are all that remain of the original homestead. The house is large and rambling. My mother was born in an upstairs bedroom. Papa moved in directly after their wedding and Adel and I both were brought home from the hospital as infants to live there. My grandmother lived with us until she died, when I was still a child.

I was raised Southern, which is to say, with the idea that a belief in God is the basis for existence. That serving one's country is noble and a just and worthy cause. And that loyalty to one's family is the foundation of civilized life. These tenets are, as Mama used to say, "the Southern gospel."

When I think back to that time, I see it as through a kaleidoscope of colors, some violent like flash fires, some soft and watercolored. Yet it isn't right to begin a history lesson in the middle of an event; instead it should be seen from a starting place of safety and security. And so this is how I first remember my history, not from scenes of chaos, upheaval and unbearable heartache, but from my place of contentment, from before my endings began. So I will go back to 1974. I had just started ninth grade with my best friend, Becky Sue Johnson.

# One
## *September 1974*

"**We** walking home together?" Becky Sue asked me as I rummaged through my locker on Friday afternoon. We had just finished up our first week of school and I was in a hurry to go.

"Only if we leave right now," I told her, slamming my locker door.

"What's the rush?" Becky eyed my stack of books. "How much homework have you got, anyway?"

Last year's testing had put me into accelerated classes, Conners' college prep program. It meant a lot more book work for me. Yet I was glad to be among about twenty in our entire school to be selected for the newly created mix of high-scoring students. I realized that it had fallen to me to do what no female in our family before me had done: go to college.

I said, "Two papers due Monday, plus a current events report for government class. Mr. Kessler wants weekly written reports about current events. He also wants everyone in his class to do a project before the end of the year."

"What are you going to do?"

"Don't know. Maybe something about Vietnam because there's lots of material about it."

"He lost a son in Vietnam. Remember? We were in fourth grade."

"I remember." Mama and Papa had gone to Jeb Kessler's funeral and to the funerals of three other young men from Conners in the following two years. "I just have to think of a good angle," I told Becky Sue. "I want an A."

Becky took two of my books and settled them onto her smaller stack. We walked out of the building together and the September heat hit me like a volleyball slammed over the net. The locals called it Indian summer. I just called it hot. The sidewalk in front of our school swarmed with kids. First graders were lined up waiting for cars to pick them up. Conners only had one school bus and it did triple duty, taking elementary kids home first, then middle-schoolers, and finally high-schoolers. I lived about six blocks from the school and Becky Sue lived two blocks farther, so we never had to ride the bus. We'd walked to and from school together ever since we were nine years old.

"Can you come to Byron's with me tomorrow?" Becky asked. "I'm going to buy Mom a birthday present."

Byron's was Conners' only department store. Short of going to Atlanta, sixty-five miles north, it was the only place to shop in our town. "I reckon," I said. "Papa's driving Mama to Atlanta tomorrow for an appointment at Emory Hospital, so I can't leave until after they're gone."

"All the way to Emory? What's wrong with Dr. Keller?"

"She's already been to Dr. Keller and he wants her to go to Emory for some tests."

"What kind of tests?"

I shrugged. "They didn't say. That puts me and Adel at the house together alone, so as you can imagine, I don't want to hang around with my sister all day. Maybe we can go to the movies after you buy your mom's present."

Two squirrels jabbered at us from overhead tree branches as we walked.

"Is Adel still going to those weekend get-togethers at the army base?"

"Hasn't missed a weekend in the past seven," I said. The training base was just outside Atlanta and was full of young soldiers, but that was about all I knew about it. That and the fact that my sister and her best friend, Sandy, drove there once a week for Red Cross–sponsored gatherings with lonely servicemen. Adel had assured our parents that there was plenty of supervision and that everything was conducted in an upright and proper manner.

There were five years and a whole lot of differences between Adel and me. Ever since her graduation, she'd been working at Papa's bank. Well, Conners Community Bank didn't really *belong* to my father, but he was responsible for running the place. He'd hired Adel for training as a teller right after she graduated from high school because it was a known fact that while my sister was beautiful, she wasn't college material.

"Bet she's got herself a boyfriend at the base," Becky said.

"Bet you're right. I mean, what would she do *without* a boyfriend to worship and adore her?"

We laughed about my sister's popularity. At school she'd been Queen of Everything and had left a string of brokenhearted boys behind her when she hadn't agreed to marry any of them. "I don't plan to stay in Conners," she'd told everyone. "I want to see the whole wide world." But to me it looked like Conners was where she'd always be. I, of course, was planning on staying in our hometown forever. I loved Conners.

A car full of boys drove past us. The driver honked the horn. J. T. Rucker, a junior and one of our high school's top football players, leaned out the window. "Hey, Boney Maroney! How's your sister? She ready for a real man?"

I felt my face flush. "You know any?" I yelled back.

"Come over here, Darcy. I'll show you my manhood."

"Get lost, you creep!"

He slapped the side of the car hard, making me jump; he laughed and the car drove off. "I really hate that guy!" I said to Becky.

"Don't judge all boys by J.T. Take Russell Danby, for instance. Don't you think he's cute?"

We'd known Russell since first grade and I'd never thought he was cute. "When did you start thinking Russell was cute?" I asked.

"Ever since third period when I dropped my pencil and he picked it up for me. When our fingers touched, I got a physical shock. I'm telling you, it went right through me. It was like I was seeing him for the first time. My heart went thump-thump and I knew he was the one I wanted."

I decided not to mention static electricity. Becky Sue was my best friend. She liked a different boy every year. She'd write his name on her notebook cover and go all flirty every time she got within ten feet of him. "So your heart thumped— that's a dead giveaway if I ever heard one."

"One day you're going to fall like a rock for

some boy and I can't wait until it happens. Then you'll see what it feels like and you won't be so skeptical of others' emotions," Becky lectured.

"Not likely," I said with a laugh. I didn't think much of any of the boys at school—they bored me. "But if it happens, you'll be the first to know."

We stopped at the place where I was to cut through the alleyway that ran behind my backyard. "Call me in the morning after your parents leave," Becky said. "Maybe we can see *The Texas Chainsaw Massacre*."

"Will do," I said. I watched her walk off, then turned, cut through a hedge, opened a tall wooden gate and stepped into paradise.

My mother's gardens were the most spectacular for their size in all of Georgia. On the acre and a half behind our house, she had created magnificent beds and planted stands of trees that had no rival. Mama urged growth from the earth the way God spilled sunlight on the South. It was said that Joy Quinlin could coax flowers from a stick poked in the ground. I believed it. She was president of the local garden club, as her mother had been before her. And it was my wish to be president of it one day too. So I read gardening books and I learned the names of every plant in the yard. I knew when they bloomed, what diseases and insects attacked them, what remedies to use to fight blights and infestations. To me, Mama's gardens were holy, and I felt closer to God when I was in the yard than when I was in church.

The yard was meticulously laid out with terraces and paths that boasted annuals, perennials, vines, bushes, a pond and a special section resplendent with a variety of roses. In the spring and throughout the summer and fall, the yard was alive with color in every shade of the rainbow. In the center of the yard, Papa had built a gazebo and a path that led to the pond. The pond was rimmed with rushes, and in the spring, water irises. Water lilies floated on the water's surface. A wooden bench beside the pond was encircled with peony and camellia bushes. Morning-glory vines spread over rocks like delicate fingers.

When I was a small child, my mother would walk me through the yard and point to the different flowers and tell me their Latin, common and sometimes old-timey folk names. She would point and say, "Now, the maiden pink attracts butterflies, Darcy." Or she'd stop in front of a particular flower to say, "Those are four-o'clocks because they only come out in the afternoon." Or, "Look, Darcy . . . there's a love-lies-bleeding."

On our garden walks, Mama used to tell me, "Angels live in gardens, Darcy."

"Where?" I would ask, looking around for the white-winged beings I saw drawn in my Sunday school papers.

"Close your eyes and breathe deep."

"All I smell is flowers, Mama," I would say.

"Not so. That's the breath of angels. And the stirrings you hear in the leaves are their wings brushing past."

When I was four, I believed her. When I was seven, I knew better. But now that I was fourteen and looking out on Mama's gardens, I again believed that angels lived here.

Whenever Mama planted, I helped. I liked to dig in the dirt—unlike Adel, who hated getting her hands dirty. The fresh loamy smell of the earth, the sound of summer rain, the scent of newly mown grass, the sight of sunlight speckling the trees sometimes brought a lump to my throat and made me want to cry for the sheer joy of seeing such beauty.

I balanced my books on my hip as I passed through the yard. Fall was coming. Despite the humid heat, I could see fall's telltale signs in the foliage of the trees and the withering clusters of summer flowers. I went up the back steps, across the screened porch and into the kitchen. I dropped my books with a thud onto the table, where Mama was sitting, sipping a cup of coffee and staring out the window.

"Don't clatter so, Darcy. You sound like a herd of elephants coming through."

"Sorry," I said. "You got a headache?" I went to the refrigerator and pulled open the door.

"No," Mama said. "And don't hold the door open. Get something and close it."

I thought Mama's behavior peculiar because she usually wanted to hear all about my school day. I would sit at the table and eat a snack, and she'd work on the beginnings of dinner while we talked. I glanced around and realized she hadn't started preparations. "What's for supper?"

"I haven't started supper yet."

"Can I fix something for you?"

Mama sighed and rose from her chair. She came around and touched my shoulder. "I didn't mean to snap at you, honey. I just have a lot on my mind. Forgive me?"

"You can be grumpy, Mama. It's allowed."

She cupped my chin, gazed down into my eyes. She looked sad, and it caused my heart to skip a beat. "I'll start supper while you talk to me," she said, turning toward the stove.

I launched into a telling of my day, but I could not forget how she had looked at me and how it had tugged at my heart.

I came to the breakfast table Saturday morning and was surprised to see Adel already there. She almost always slept in on Saturdays. Papa was reading the paper and Mama was making waffles. "Morning," Papa said.

I scraped the chair across the linoleum and Adel shot me an intolerant glare. "Morning, all. Missing out on your beauty sleep, aren't you, Adel?"

"I slept fine," she said. "Although I don't know how. Your radio blared half the night."

"I fell asleep with it on. Sorry."

Our rooms were down the hall from each other. Adel had claimed Grandmother's big upstairs bedroom after she died. I had been eight, and up until that time Adel and I had shared the smaller, middle bedroom. Adel's room had its own bathroom, while I used the one across the hall, which was just as well because she kept drawers full of cosmetics, hair sprays and perfumes. There would have been no room for my meager collection of stuff. Yet when Adel had moved out, I felt adrift and lonely. "I need the space," she had told me, then shut the door and left me to grow up on my own.

Mama and Papa's room was over the back porch, part of the new addition to the house when they'd married. Their space was far away from the noise of Adel's and my rooms and had large windows that looked down into the backyard gardens.

Papa folded his paper and buttered the waffle

Mama had put on his plate. "We'll be staying over in Atlanta tonight," he said. "Adel, I expect you to take care of your sister."

"But Sandy and I are going to the dance at the base tonight. It's all planned."

"Can't be helped," Papa said. "You're responsible for fixing supper and breakfast tomorrow."

"I don't need her to *baby*-sit," I said indignantly. "I'm fourteen!" I sure didn't want Adel sulking around and being hateful to me for twenty-four hours because she couldn't keep her date.

"It's not open for discussion," Papa said in the voice he used when he was finished with a topic. He cut his waffle with the side of his fork and took a mouthful.

Adel and I exchanged desperate glances, each for different reasons. "Becky Sue asked me to spend the night and I said I'd check with Mama, but that I figured it would be all right," I blurted out. While it wasn't exactly the truth, Becky and I had been having sleepovers since the third grade and our presence in each other's families was frequent and interchangeable. "Can I, Mama? That way Adel can keep her date and Mrs. Johnson can watch out for me."

"We'll have the car," Papa said.

"Sandy's driving," Adel said quickly.

"It's all right, Graham." Mama interrupted

our negotiation. "Probably be easier that way. We won't have to worry about Darcy and Adel pecking at each other."

Papa glowered at both me and Adel. "Never could understand why the two of you can't get along. You're sisters."

"We get along fine," Adel said, giving me a look that was more grateful than dismissive because my quick thinking had saved her plans.

Of course, I was doing it out of self-preservation. Everybody knows that a peeved Adel is worse than a roomful of hostile bees.

# Two

"What are you going to buy your mom?" I asked Becky Sue. We'd just stepped into Byron's, where the air felt cool against my skin after our half-mile walk downtown in the muggy morning heat.

"Something on the sale racks," Becky said. "I'm broke."

We went to the women's area of the store and started sorting through the clothes. Most were leftovers from the summer and looked pretty tired. "How about this?" I held up a red-and-white-checked gingham blouse. "It's not very much."

"She'll look like a tablecloth," Becky said, continuing her search. "What do you think's wrong with your mama?"

"It's just tests."

"But all the way to Emory—"

"I'm worried enough about it, Becky Sue. So stop talking about it, all right?"

Becky shrugged off my sharp tone. "Well, at least Adel's out of your immediate future."

It was Becky's way of reminding me that she had rescued me by letting me spend the day and night with her and so I didn't need to snap. I said, "I'm sure about Adel seeing a guy at the base. The minute Mama and Papa drove off, she shut her room door and started primping. She'd have been snarling at me all day long."

That was my way of saying thank you to Becky for rescuing me.

Becky Sue held up another blouse. "This looks like Mom, but it's too small."

We resumed our search. By lunchtime we'd bought Mrs. Johnson a purse and were eating lunch at the Woolworth soda counter. "You coming to teen group Sunday night?" Becky Sue asked me.

"I reckon so. Adel's got choir, but I don't think Mama and Papa will go to church after the drive home. You be there?" Our families were members of the First Baptist Church on Main Street, which was two blocks from the Second Baptist Church on Main Street. Mama's kin had been members at the First Baptist Church since the 1860s. It was where Mama and Papa got married. I practically grew up in the pews—Baptists went to church every Sunday morning, Sunday night, Wednesday night for potluck supper and all week long during Lent and revival meetings.

"I wouldn't miss Pastor Jim's guitar picking for anything," Becky Sue said.

The church had started a group for teens in 1971 and invited a nice young pastor just out of seminary, Jim Murphy, and his wife, Carole, to come to Conners to assist old Pastor Franklin, who was fixing to retire but hadn't yet. Pastor Jim was young and full of ideas and we kids liked him. Mama had taken Carole under her wing because Carole grew up in Chicago and didn't exactly understand all our Southern ways, which Mama said were above anyone's total understanding.

It was generally assumed that Baptists didn't drink, dance, swear, play cards or go to the movies, but times were changing, and according to Mama, while drinking and swearing were still off-limits, we'd slowly absorbed the other sins into our daily lives, *and* without incident. That was how Adel got away with going to events at the military base, where everybody knew there was dancing. "Dancing won't do any harm," Mama had told the clacking tongues in the garden club. "Why, Jesus himself might have danced at the wedding in Cana. The Bible doesn't say otherwise." The old guard didn't approve, but people liked Mama, so she got away with things others in Conners didn't.

I took a long sip of my vanilla milk shake. "Carole cornered Mama at the supper Wednesday night and I just happened to overhear something she said." I paused for dramatic effect. "I think it's supposed to be a secret."

"What?" Becky rose to the bait.

"Maybe I shouldn't say."

"You better say! Or I'll have Mom call Adel and say you can't sleep over."

I smiled. It was fun getting Becky Sue riled up. "Okay, no need to threaten me." I glanced around to make sure no one was eavesdropping, then leaned close to Becky's face. "I heard Carole tell Mama that her and Pastor Jim's lives were taking a real turn. Seems like they're getting an addition to their family."

Becky looked properly surprised. "They're having a baby?"

"A seventeen-year-old baby," I said. "I heard Carole say that her kid brother is in all kinds of trouble up in Chicago and that in order to keep him out of *jail*"—I emphasized the word for effect—"she and Pastor Jim were having him come live with them."

Becky Sue's eyes grew wide, then narrowed. "Are you making that up? 'Cause if you are . . ."

"Cross my heart," I said.

"When's he coming?"

"Didn't hear that part. I just know he is coming."

"Wonder if he's cute," Becky said.

I rolled my eyes. "I thought your sights were set on Russell."

"I wouldn't want to pass up a good opportunity. That is, *if* Carole's brother is worth looking at."

"He's a proven troublemaker and probably homely to boot."

"Why should he be homely? Carole's pretty."

"So's Adel," I countered. "But that doesn't make me pretty."

Becky Sue measured me with her gaze. "You're passable. Tall and skinny and flat as a board, but passable."

I felt my face turning red, knowing I'd stupidly left myself open for Becky's critique. My build was a sore spot to me. At fourteen, I still lacked the bumps and curves that every other girl in ninth grade had. Mama called me "slow to bloom, just like late summer roses." But Adel said I'd never bloom because I was too thorny. Truth was, I believed Adel.

Becky must have sensed my discomfort because she quickly added, "Magazine models are tall and slim. Maybe you'll be one someday."

"I doubt that," I said, sliding off the stool. "Come on, let's go to the movie."

We paid our bill, then walked outside and across the street, with Becky Sue chattering all the way and me deep into my own thoughts about myself and what was going on with my mother.

I called home Sunday after church because Adel hadn't shown up for the eleven-o'clock service. "I got home late last night," she told me.

"Papa won't like knowing you skipped church," I said.

"And he won't know unless someone opens her big mouth."

"They say when they'll be home?" I ignored her threat.

"I expect they'll be here late this afternoon."

"Then I'm staying over here at Becky's. We'll go to teen group together. Will you be at choir practice?"

"I'll be there. You're not my conscience, you know," she added.

"Never wanted to be," I said. "But the one God gave you seems to be on vacation." I hung up before she could blast me.

Teen group met in a downstairs room off the

kitchen area. The room held two old sofas, some overstuffed chairs and a collection of vinyl bean-bags, plus some folding chairs. Pastor Jim played the guitar and led us in some songs. Carole passed around a platter of cookies and I settled into a beanbag next to Becky's.

"I have some exciting news," Carole said. Her face was flushed and she looked more anxious than excited. "My seventeen-year-old brother, Jason Polwalski, is coming for an extended visit next weekend."

I poked Becky Sue in the ribs and gave her an I-told-you-so glance. All the other kids kept politely silent.

Carole continued. "Jason will be a senior and I would appreciate it if each and every one of you would welcome him and make him feel like a part of the Conners community. I know you all understand how difficult it might be to start in a new school without your friends." She made eye contact with several of the jocks and more popular kids. "So, I'm asking you as a personal favor to me and Pastor Jim to help Jason find acceptance from this caring Christian community."

I almost laughed out loud. Some of these kids were about as friendly as vipers. Conners had a pecking order, and because our town was so small, cliques weren't easy to penetrate. Around these parts, newcomers had to work their way into people's affections, and the regulars had to warm up to them. I hoped the link with Pastor Jim and Carole would be enough but guessed that Jason was going to have to struggle for a while to belong. Maybe Jason was a jock. That would help. Football players were worshiped as minor gods. If Jason could run, punt or pass, I figured he had a chance.

"She didn't say a word about *why* Jason's coming," Becky Sue whispered to me when the meeting had broken up after our Bible study on the Good Samaritan.

"And don't you say a word about it either," I warned. "It's supposed to be a secret."

"I never would," Becky insisted. "Hope Carole's told the chief of police, though."

"Unkind," I said.

"What are you two whispering about? Did I hear the word 'police'?" J. T. Rucker asked from behind us.

I jumped a foot and that made him laugh. In my frostiest tone, I said, "None of your business."

He feigned fear. "What are you going to do? Sock me?"

Murder had crossed my mind on more than one occasion when it came to J.T. He might have been the defensive center for the Conners football team and about the size of a tank, but I considered him dumb as a rock and mean as a junkyard dog. I'd always been grateful that he was older than me and that I'd never had to tolerate him in a classroom. "You know, you're one of the main people Carole was talking to about being nice to her brother," I told him.

"I'll be nice." J.T. had a glint in his eye that said different.

"I'll just bet you will," I said.

"Do you know this guy?"

"No."

"Then why are you so hot on looking out for him?"

"I'm not!"

"I'll bet you've seen his picture and you'd like to jump his bones."

I felt my face getting red. Why did I always blush in times of pressure? "I know Carole and I like her and she asked real nice for us to be accepting and—"

"Do you know your face gets all red and blotchy when you get angry?"

I balled up my fist, but Becky Sue said, "Church," and I remembered where we were.

J.T. began to laugh and I stalked off, angrier than I'd been in days. Becky Sue followed me, saying, "Why do you let him get to you like that?"

"I don't plan on it," I said, hurrying up the stairs and into the narthex. "It just happens because he's such a jerk."

"He's always been a jerk. But he held Branson back from making a touchdown last week. Won the game for us in a way."

"And that's supposed to excuse him from acting like a human being?"

"There you are!" Adel pushed through the wooden inner doors of the sanctuary. Other choir members began to fill the narthex behind her. "Come on. Mrs. Becker is giving us a ride home."

"I'm going with Becky Sue," I said. "My stuff's still at her house."

"You can get it later. Papa called just before I came to practice and said he and Mama were on their way home and that when they arrived they wanted to talk to us. Together," she added before I could say a word.

"What about?"

"They didn't say. But it sounded important."

"I'll leave your things by your front door," Becky said as Adel all but dragged me out.

I followed Adel to the parking lot and got into Mrs. Becker's car. "You doing all right, Darcy?" Mrs. Becker asked.

"Just fine," I lied. I wasn't doing fine at all.

At the house, I saw our car in the driveway and ran up the walk ahead of Adel. In the kitchen, Mama was sitting at the table and her eyes looked as if she'd been crying. Papa was sitting beside her, but he stood when we came into the room. "Hold up, girls."

"What's wrong?" Adel asked.

He and Mama exchanged glances.

I went all cold and clammy. "You all right, Mama?"

She shook her head. "I have to go back to Emory, girls . . . on Wednesday," she said, her voice a bit hoarse from crying. "I—I have to have an operation."

# Three

⤬ ⤬

"What kind of operation?" Adel got the question out before I could.

Papa put his hand on Mama's shoulder and she reached up and squeezed his fingers. "It seems I have a lump in my left breast," she said.

A shockwave went over me. For starters, I had never heard my mother use the word "breast" in a sentence unless it followed the words "Thanksgiving turkey" or "cut-up frying chicken."

Adel's sharp intake of breath told me this was bad news that she understood better than I.

"Wh-what's that mean?" I asked. My voice trembled.

Tears filled Mama's eyes. "Now, please, girls, let me get through this before we fall apart." She cleared her throat. "I found the lump myself while I was taking a shower. I went to Dr. Keller last week and he said I needed a mammogram and that the closest facility with such a machine was at Emory. It's a kind of X-ray machine that takes pictures of the breast. I had the pictures taken yesterday and that's when the doctor saw the lump clearly."

Yesterday I had been shopping with Becky, sorting through sale racks, eating lunch and going to the movies without a care in the world while my mother was facing this terrible news.

"Is it big?" Adel asked.

"Big enough," Mama said. "But now that we know it's there, the doctors must take it out."

That made sense to me. "When?" Adel asked.

"The surgery's on Thursday. That's why I'm checking in on Wednesday. Afterward, I'll be in the hospital recovering. That will take a week or more, depending on how I do."

"A whole week?" I blurted out, dismayed. "But it's just a lump."

Adel gave me a hard look. Mama's expression was kinder. "If it's a bad lump . . ." Mama's voice faltered. "If it's—"

"Cancer." Papa filled in the word Mama couldn't bring herself to say.

I recoiled. I'd heard of cancer. People died from cancer.

"What will they do, Mama, if the lump is bad?" I felt cold and numb.

She said nothing.

Adel said, "Please tell us everything, Mama. Don't hold anything back from us. Please."

Mama crossed her arms as if to shield herself. "A mastectomy. Surgeons remove the entire breast and some lymph nodes from under the arm."

I knew a little about lymph nodes from health and hygiene classes. The lymph system made white blood cells, and their job was to fight germs. Why hadn't her white cells just attacked the cancer and destroyed it?

"Why do they take out lymph nodes?" I asked, determined to hear every detail of this terrible operation.

"To see if the cancer has metastasized."

I didn't know what that word meant, but I wasn't about to ask because it was evident by the expression on Adel's face that she *did* know and that it wasn't a good thing. I was still reeling from the information about Mama having her entire breast removed because of one lump.

"But the lump might not be cancer," I said, sounding hopeful. "It could be just a common, ordinary, everyday garden-variety lump."

Mama nodded. "That is my hope."

My head spun with information and words no one should have to hear. I wanted to cry but didn't dare. It might tell Mama that I didn't have faith that her lump was nothing at all.

Adel circled the table and crouched in front of Mama. "This can't be happening to you. It just can't be." She laid her head in Mama's lap, and Mama stroked her hair.

My sister was right. People as wonderful as my mother did not have horrible things like cancer happen to them. Mama was good and kind and loved by everyone who knew her.

"That's what I've been telling myself ever since I saw Dr. Keller, but unfortunately it is happening to me. To all of us, in a way."

"Which brings me to our next topic," Papa said. "What's happening to your mother is family business. I don't want tongues wagging all over town about this. It isn't gossip."

"I'll be telling people," Mama said. "But at my own choosing."

"But people know you went to Emory today for tests. Becky and Mrs. Johnson—"

Mama held up her hand. "You may say that the tests are inconclusive and that I will be returning to Emory midweek for more tests."

I nodded. "All right, Mama."

Adel pulled away, found a tissue and wiped her eyes. "I want to be there for your surgery, Mama," she said.

"You have a job."

"I'll quit."

"Well, if Adel's going, so am I," I said.

"Excuse me," Papa interrupted, his face in a scowl. "Did I just hear you two *sass?*"

"It's all right, Graham," Mama said. "This is hard news for all of us. I see no harm in the girls' coming. It might do me good to wake up and see my family around me if . . ." She paused. "Well, if the news isn't good."

"But it will be good news, Mama," I said with conviction. "I know it will."

We talked some more, but when Adel and I went upstairs, I grabbed her arm. "Adel, I don't know what that word 'metastasize' means."

"It means 'spread.' It means that cancer has spread into other parts of a person's body."

Later in my room, I lay in bed and gazed through the window, staring up at a sliver of the moon peeking from the sky. The night was silent, my room dark, the house quiet and the night air heavy with the scent of a fading summer garden. I folded my hands together and whispered, *Please, God, let my mama be all right. Don't let it be cancer. Don't let it have already spread.*

We left for Atlanta Wednesday afternoon in the rain, with Papa driving our 1972 Ford Fairlane, Mama in the front beside him, me and Adel in the backseat. Each of us had packed a small bag because we'd be staying overnight. My teachers had all given me excused absences, and I'd told only Becky Sue about Mama's tests and that she had to return for more. I knew Becky Sue would tell others, and I knew she suspected I wasn't telling her everything, but to her credit, she did not pry.

Going to Atlanta was usually a fun event because Mama would take us shopping for back-to-school clothes and sometimes, time permitting, Christmas presents. We hadn't gone this year before school started because Adel was working and I didn't care all that much about fashion, so Mama had ordered a few things out of the Sears catalog for me.

The hospital was located on the campus of Emory University, and I stared with fascination at students walking along the sidewalks and going in and out of buildings. It did not seem possible to me that my classroom work back in Conners would prepare me to become a student at any college in only four more years. And yet that was what I had decided to do—leave home and go to college. I began to rethink my commitment and wondered if Papa would mind having two daughters working at his bank should I drop out of the college-prep program.

The entrance lobby of the hospital looked

more like the formal room in an old mansion, with fancy carpets and hanging chandeliers. But once we turned the corner, everything changed and we were in sterile-looking hallways with walls painted mint green and smelling of antiseptics and pine cleaners.

We checked my mother into a private room on the fifth floor, and once she was settled in her bed, we were allowed in to see her.

"My surgeon, Dr. Willingham, will be in after supper," Mama told us. "He'll operate first thing in the morning."

I wanted to see this man, the one who had permission to cut off my mother's breast, but I was fearful that I might kick and scratch him simply because he would dare to touch her.

Mama took Papa's hand. "You take the girls to supper and check into the hotel. I'll be fine. Truth is, I'm a bit tired and believe I will sleep a little."

We kissed her goodbye and Papa drove us to a Howard Johnson motel not too far from the campus, where he had reserved two rooms. Papa was in one room and Adel and I in the other; we would share a double bed. We ate in the motel restaurant, but it was plain to see that none of us had an appetite. Eating out was a rare occurrence for us, and usually enjoyed, but tonight the mashed potatoes and meat loaf stuck in my throat.

Back in the room, I watched Adel going through her nightly rituals while I sat cross-legged on the bed, hugging a pillow to my chest. We hadn't spoken since we'd said good night to Papa, and I could not stand the sad silence any longer. "It's not going to be cancer, is it, Adel?"

She was brushing her long black hair and her gaze caught mine in the mirror. "That's what the operation will tell us," she said.

"But don't you have faith that it won't be cancer?"

"I don't reckon that my faith will change it one way or the other. It either is, or it isn't. God's already decided that."

"Well, I don't think it is. I think it's just a false alarm." I kept my tone confident because Adel's lack of confidence scared me. And I sure didn't want her to rile God with her lack of faith.

She turned to face me. "Grandmother died from this, Darcy. Didn't you know?"

I stared at her, slack-jawed. "Grandmother had breast cancer?"

"She never recovered from the operation. But she was old," Adel added hastily. "Mama's a whole lot younger."

I tried to remember those days before Grandmother's funeral. I recalled her being hospitalized, but I hadn't had a clue as to what was wrong with her. What I remembered most were my mother's

tears and the dark, ominous wreath that had hung
on our front door after Grandmother had died.
"Poor Grandmother," I said.

Adel slid into the bed, reached up and flipped
the switch on the bedside lamp. Out of the darkness, she said, "Doctors think it runs in families.
That it can be passed along."

If that was true, then Mama might have been
cursed from before she was born.

Adel and I lay there in the dark without
touching, our backs to one another, each curled
up in a ball. I felt tears fill my eyes, and I stuffed a
fistful of the wadded sheet into my mouth so that
I could cry quietly. It was a long time before I realized that Adel had done the same thing and that
she was crying too.

We were at the hospital by seven the next
morning. The nurses had already given Mama a
sedative, and she was groggy. "You sleep good,
Joy?" Papa asked, kissing her forehead.

"They kept . . . waking me up," Mama said.
Her speech sounded slurred. "Hi, girls. You . . .
two get a good . . . night's . . . sleep?"

We assured her we had. I asked, "How long
will this operation take, Mama?"

"Dr. Willingham said about . . . an hour if the
lump is . . . just . . . a lump." Her voice floated up
like petals on water.

The clock on the wall read 7:30. I held her hand.

A man swooped into the room pushing a gurney. "Morning, Mrs. Quinlin. I'm Nigel and I'm here to take you down to the OR. Ready?"

"Don't know . . . if I'll ever be . . . ready," Mama sighed.

He helped her scoot onto the rolling bed, transferred her IV line and headed out the door. We walked beside the bed as he pushed it down the hall. At the elevator, Nigel said, "There's a family waiting room down the hall. Or you can wait in her room. The surgeon will call you when she's in recovery."

The doors closed and the three of us stood staring in disbelief, like people watching a bus that had left them behind. "Let's wait in her room," Papa said.

Papa had arranged for a television to be put into Mama's room, and the *Today Show* was playing. Hosts Jim Hartz and Barbara Walters were introducing newscaster Frank Blair. The anchorman reported the latest world events, and the big story was about how President Ford had offered clemency to Vietnam War draft dodgers. Footage of helicopters and foot soldiers and fiery jungles played, then cut to video of protesters marching with antiwar signs and shouting, "Hell no! We won't go!" as the reporter talked. Clemency meant that anyone who'd refused to fight in the war could come home again without being arrested or fined. Like my childhood games, the President was calling, "All-y, all-y, in free."

Adel stared at the small TV screen and its images of war and I saw tears in her eyes.

"That doesn't seem right," Papa said, for he was watching too. "Our boys died in those jungles and over here they burned our flag and spit on all our government stands for. Now Mr. Ford says it doesn't matter. That those cowards can skulk back home and join daily life like nothing ever happened. I've been to too many funerals of boys who loved their country and did their duty to think this is right." I knew Papa's Southern sense of justice was offended. "But what should I expect from a man who pardoned Richard Nixon?" he added with disgust.

Fascinated, I watched as dark helicopters rose over burning jungles. It was all so far away from Georgia's red clay and my life in Conners. And from my mother lying on an operating table under a surgeon's knife. Mama also was fighting a war. Only God could grant her clemency.

When the phone in the room finally rang, I jumped to my feet. Papa took the receiver, listened, said, "Thank you, Doctor," and hung up. "Your mother's in recovery and awake," he told us. "We can go see her."

I quickly looked at the clock and saw that almost three hours had passed since Nigel had taken Mama to the operating room. I got a sick feeling in my stomach. Three hours gone meant that the lump had not been friendly and my mother had lost her breast.

# Four

The recovery room held several patients, all bedded down behind white curtains. I don't know why I thought Mama would be the only person there and that a troop of nurses would be hovering around her bed, but that was not the case. She lay with IVs in her arm and wires that led to a machine keeping track of her heartbeat. We crowded around her bed like boats around an island searching for safe harbor before a storm. I could see a bandage at the neck of her hospital gown.

"Hi," Mama said. "It's all over." Her voice sounded hoarse and her lips looked parched.

"You did fine, Joy," Papa said.

"I know the truth," Mama said. "I have cancer."

"You *had* cancer," I whispered. "They cut it out."

"The surgeon said it'll take some time before the full pathology report comes back from the lab."

Papa leaned over and cupped her cheek. "Don't you go worrying about it, you hear? Right now, you just rest and get your strength back. We'll be waiting for you in your room."

Her eyes filled with tears. "I love you all so much."

"We love you too," Adel said, tears running down her cheeks.

I longed to throw my arms around my mother and not let go, but the tubes and wires and her frailty overwhelmed me. I wanted to run far away from this place where pain-filled voices calling out to nurses for relief floated around the room like whispering ghosts. I wanted time to absorb the bad news, to think about this plague that had fallen on my mother so undeservedly.

"Come on, girls," Papa said. "Let's let your mother rest."

I fled the recovery room ahead of the others.

On Friday morning Mama was sitting up in bed when we came to visit. Her left arm was wrapped in an Ace bandage and held up by pulleys anchored to a contraption next to her bed. "To keep the swelling down," she told us. Long tubes were visible under her bedclothes.

"Drainage tubes," she explained. "The nurses empty them a couple times a day. And they change the bandages too."

I saw Adel shudder, but I didn't let on that it affected me one bit.

"I'll be taking the girls home today. Then I'll be coming back to stay awhile," Papa said.

"But your job—" Mama started.

"Will be there waiting for me when this is all over," Papa finished. "I'm the boss, remember?"

Both Adel and I protested being taken home, but Papa wouldn't put up with it. "There is nothing for the two of you to do here. Your mother needs her rest and you both have obligations. I expect you both to stay at home and carry on life as usual. I will bring your mother home when the doctor says I can. In the meantime, I will call home every night and we can talk to one another."

I expected Adel to persuade Papa otherwise. She had strategies for getting her way with him, but now, when I was counting on her to use her bag of tricks, she just nodded and agreed to his mandates. "We'll keep things in order," she said.

Out in the hall, Papa looked me in the eye and said, "Adel is in charge."

I started to protest. Papa didn't give me a chance.

"I don't want your mother to worry one iota

about what's going on in her house. I expect the house to be clean, meals prepared, clothes washed and squabbling kept to a minimum. Do I make myself clear?"

"Yes, Papa," I said, torn between wanting to object and knowing better.

"Say your goodbyes to your mama, and let's get going. It's a long drive."

We did and it was all I could do to keep from bawling. Papa told Mama he'd see her Saturday around lunchtime and kissed her goodbye. Finally, we left Emory and headed out of Atlanta toward Conners, leaving Mama behind. It hardly seemed like a week had passed since I'd stood in the school halls talking to Becky Sue about homework and setting plans for the weekend. Just a single week gone out of September 1974, yet somehow I felt years older. And a whole lot sadder.

After breakfast on Saturday, Papa packed and left. Adel and I stood on the veranda and watched his car disappear around the corner. "Come on," Adel said. "We've got chores."

Her bossing me was starting already, and Papa not gone two minutes. "I thought I'd work in the yard," I said politely. "You know how Mama loves her gardens, and they need tending."

To my surprise, Adel said, "That's a good idea. I'll start in the house."

The weather was cooler and the sun was shining as I walked to the garden shed and dragged out tools. I set to work pruning the butterfly bushes, Latin name *Buddleia*, and clipping the dead and dying clusters off the hydrangeas. I was making a mental list of what I had to do to keep the gardens beautiful until Mama could work them again when Becky Sue came around the corner of the house.

"Hey," she said. "I waited as long as I could before coming over. How's your mama?"

Without warning, big tears welled up in my eyes. I dropped the pruning shears and wiped them away with the sleeve of my shirt. "She has cancer, Becky Sue," I said, not giving a minute's thought to Papa's admonishments about keeping family business private. Not that it was going to be easy. All of Mama's friends from church and the garden club had been calling nonstop. Word had already gotten around town that she was at Emory.

Becky started crying too. "Oh, Darcy, I'm sorry," she wailed. "This is terrible. Just awful."

We walked out to the gazebo together and sat on the wooden bench swing suspended by chains from the ceiling. "She's being real brave," I said. "But I'm scared."

"Course you are. My grandpa died of cancer."

"Thank you for that information," I said, not too kindly.

Becky slapped her hand over her mouth. "Sorry. Had no call to say that. Grandpa was old and sick for a long time. He smoked too, and that's what probably gave him lung cancer. So he sort of brought it on himself."

"Mama didn't do nothing to bring breast cancer on herself." I scuffed my old gardening shoes on the wood flooring. "It's not fair, Becky. Not fair at all."

"You coming to school on Monday, or going back to the hospital?"

"Papa says we have to carry on like nothing's wrong. I don't care a thing about school right now." I crossed my arms in defiance but after a few minutes asked, "So what have I missed since Wednesday?"

"J.T. got into a fight behind the gym with Billy Harrold Friday after school. Seems as if Billy was flirting with Donna and J.T. took exception to it."

"That girl's a born troublemaker," I said. Donna McGowen was pretty but didn't have the good sense of a grasshopper. She wasn't happy unless a boy was mooning over her. She and J.T. had been on and off together for years. "I hope they make each other miserable, because they truly deserve each other," I said. "Anything else?"

"I heard Carole and Jim are picking up that brother of hers at the Atlanta airport today,"

Becky said. "So I'm figuring he'll be at teen group tomorrow night. You'll come, won't you?"

I was curious about Jason, and I sort of felt sorry for him, being forced to come live with his sister. Kids never got much say-so about life. Someone was forever telling us what to do or not to do. "I'll be there," I said. Silently, I vowed to be nice to him. Mama would say it was the Christian thing to do. I just figured that misery would love some company.

After church on Sunday, Adel fixed dinner, always a big family meal at our house, and the two of us sat in the dining room mostly staring at our plates, neither of us having an appetite. "Meat's dry," I said.

"Put some gravy on it," Adel said.

The gravy was lumpy, but I thought it best to keep that to myself. Just then, the phone rang and Adel groaned. "Will you get that?" she asked. "I just don't think I can listen to one more well-wishing, good-intentioned friend wanting information about Mama going to the hospital."

I jumped up and went to the kitchen, where the downstairs phone hung on the wall. I answered it and a deep male voice asked, "Is Adel there?"

Now, men calling Adel was nothing new to

me, except that this voice didn't sound like anyone's I'd heard before. It had an odd, non-
Southern accent. "Who may I say is calling?" I
asked in my most polite manner.

He said, "Barry. That is, Specialist Fourth
Class Barry Sorenson."

A *soldier*. "This is her sister, Darcy," I said,
again using my best voice. "Just a minute and I'll
get Adel."

When I told her who was on the phone, Adel
let out a little squeal and ran for the stairs. "I'll
take it upstairs," she said. I returned to the
kitchen and passed the news on to Barry. Seconds
later, Adel came on the line. "Hi. How are you?"
she said in a breathless, sexy voice. I cringed but
didn't hang up. I'd seen my sister trot out her
charm many times before and thought it sugary
and nauseating.

"Hi to you," Barry said. "I missed you at the
club last night. I was wondering if you are all
right."

"I—wait a minute. Darcy, if you are still on
that phone, hang up this instant. This is a *personal*
conversation." Adel's instructions sounded sharp
and demanding.

"I'm hanging up," I told her, taking my sweet
time. "Bye, Barry. Nice talking to you."

I had something to tell Becky Sue. Something

that didn't involve my mother or any sadness. Adel had a soldier boy hooked on her line. I wondered just how long it would take for her to reel him in.

That evening Carole stopped me in the hall just outside the teen room. "Darcy, Jim and I went to see your mother after we met Jason's plane yesterday. She seems in good spirits."

Carole was only six years older than Adel, and Mama had taken Carole under her wing. Carole was shy and, I learned later, scared about even coming to the South, what with stories about violence over desegregation standard fare on Northern newscasts when she was growing up. Which weren't true for the most part. Why, everybody in Conners went to school together, blacks and whites, and nobody ever thought twice about it. And the thing I'd learned was that there were some nice black kids and some mean ones, but not one of them, black or white, was as hateful as J. T. Rucker. Anyway, Mama let Carole start a ladies' Bible study in our house because Carole needed confidence, and women would come to Mama's house just because Mama said so. Soon everybody thought the world of Carole and she fit right in with our town.

Now, looking at Carole, I could see that my

mother's troubles were affecting her deeply. "It must have meant a lot to Mama to see a friendly face from home," I said. "Thank you."

"We all held hands and prayed for her quick and complete recovery. It was a comfort to both of us." She patted my hand. "Joy's a wonderful woman, and I know God must have big plans for her."

I hoped God had told this to Carole directly, because he wasn't saying much to me about my mother. "Thank you," I repeated. "Becky told me Jason was coming tonight."

Carole sighed. "Yes, but under protest."

From the room, we heard guitar music, which meant that Pastor Jim had started the meeting. We went inside, and I stepped over kids sitting on the floor in order to sink down beside Becky. I saw Jason instantly. He was sitting by himself, his back against the wall, and he didn't look happy. He wore a worn leather jacket and jeans—and nobody wore jeans to church, so he really looked out of place. His hair was straight and light brown and too long, his skin tanner than I'd have imagined for someone living in Chicago. His gaze flicked over us and I saw that his eyes were bright green and intense, his lips full, his expression defiant. I liked his looks and thought his sharp, angular features attractive, almost dangerous looking. My cheeks began to feel warm and I looked away, afraid someone would see the effect he was having on me.

Becky leaned toward me. "Cute, isn't he?" she whispered in my ear.

"Passable," I said.

After several songs, Pastor Jim put down his guitar and introduced Jason. "As most of you know by now, Carole's brother, Jason Polwalski, will be living with us and attending Conners High School this year. I hope all of you will make him feel welcome."

We waved and greeted him politely as a group. Jason surveyed us coolly. Jim cleared his throat and I could tell he wasn't thrilled with Jason's less-than-enthusiastic response to us. "We're going to continue our Bible study in Luke," Jim said. "If you'll open your Bibles to Luke Eleven . . ."

Without a word, Jason stood up and walked out of the room.

I looked for Jason in the halls at school on Monday but didn't see him until after lunch. He stood out from the regulars. His clothes were wrong and his expression continually said *Back off.* Over the next several days, I thought about ways to reach out to him but kept drawing a blank. I was a lowly ninth grader and he was a senior. Besides, every time I saw him, I had strange reactions. My palms perspired, my heart raced, and my face felt warm, like I might be catching something. I'd never experienced such things around a boy before, so I didn't quite know how to handle it. I could have talked it over with Becky Sue but figured she might take to teasing me about it, and I sure didn't want that!

I was in my room doing homework, thinking over Jason and smelling the burnt aroma of supper being prepared by my sister, when she yelled, "Darcy! Come down here quick and see what the news is saying."

I bolted down the stairs and into the living room, where Adel stood in front of the television. There on the screen, in living color, sat Walter Cronkite, and he was saying that Betty Ford, wife of our President, Gerald Ford, had been diagnosed with breast cancer and would undergo surgery.

Adel and I looked at each other in utter amazement. It was September 30, and the wife of our country's President was going through the same thing our mama was going through. Breast cancer was a scourge and definitely no respecter of persons. It had attacked two fine women, and I was certain that I knew what Betty Ford's family was feeling at the moment. They were frightened. Same as us.

# Five
## *October*

≈≈   ≈≈

"Jason has a motorcycle," Becky Sue told me on Wednesday as we were walking home from school. "I saw him riding it into the school parking lot this morning from my homeroom window. He was tardy."

"Really?" I said. It made him all the more interesting to me because motorcycle riders were unusual in Conners. We all lusted after our own car, but few families had more than one. Mostly the kids in our school drove beat-up pickup trucks, shared the family car or rode in groups in friends' cars. Usually only troublemakers rode motorcycles. "So do you think you'd like to take a ride on it?" I wanted to get Becky's reaction.

"Are you serious? My daddy would kill me if I ever got on a motorcycle. How about you?"

"What Papa doesn't know won't hurt me," I

said, letting her know that if I ever got the chance, I would take it. "I'm sure it's a one-in-a-million shot anyway. He keeps to himself." Nobody at school was friendly to him. Not even me, but that was mostly because my tongue stuck to the roof of my mouth whenever I was near him, which was rarely.

"Russell told me that J.T. and his football buddies stole Jason's gym clothes yesterday so he couldn't dress out. Coach chewed him out in front of the whole class. Really embarrassed Jason."

I felt offended for Jason's sake. "J.T. is such a royal pain. And after Pastor Jim made a special request for us to treat Jason nice. Why is J.T. such a jerk?"

"Does he need an excuse? How's your mama?" Becky Sue changed the subject.

"Papa's bringing her home today." And was I ever ready to have her home. Adel had done a passable job of keeping the house in order, but I was about starved for Mama's cooking. During the week gone by, I'd eaten more food singed around its edges than I cared to think about.

By suppertime, Papa hadn't shown up, so Adel and I sat down to more of her pitiful cooking. I poked the lump of meat on my plate with my fork. "What is it?"

"Pork chop," she said.

"Do the pigs know how bad you're treating their kin?"

"Just eat it."

"I can't cut it," I said.

Adel opened her mouth to blast me, but just then the phone rang. She threw down her fork, saying, "I'll get it." She hurried to the kitchen.

"Saved by the bell," I muttered. She always ran for the phone now and I figured it was because she was hoping for another call from her soldier boy, Barry. When she didn't return, I made another stab—literally—at eating the pork chop. "Poor fellow," I said to the slab of overcooked meat, not sure if I was pitying the chop or the soldier.

Finally Adel came to the table. She looked upset. "That was Papa," she said. "He's not coming back tonight, and neither is Mama. Her doctors want her to start radiation and chemotherapy treatments."

"What!" I could hardly contain my disappointment. "But why?"

Adel shook her head and I could see she was pretty upset. "It's just what they have to do now. To make sure the cancer's killed."

"You telling me everything?"

"I'm telling you what Papa said. She starts radiation tomorrow. Chemo next week."

"How long?"

"A month to six weeks."

I was so shocked, I sputtered, "Six weeks! That's forever!"

"Papa said he'll be home tomorrow after her first treatment and that he'll take us to visit this weekend."

"Why can't she come home to have radiation and chemo?"

"Conners doesn't have the equipment for radiation treatments, and Mama has to get the treatments five days a week. And the chemo is no walk in the park either. She's better off staying near the hospital at Emory."

I knew that what Adel was saying was true, because ours was a small town with one doctor, a dentist who only came through twice a week and one emergency medical care clinic run by Dr. Keller, the lone doctor. If a person wasn't bleeding or in danger of dying quickly, he had to go to a hospital in either Atlanta to the north or Macon to the south. I began to see that despite my fondness for my hometown, Conners had some shortcomings. "So she's just going to live in the hospital?" I felt cheated.

"Papa said she'll become an outpatient. He said that private homes around the area rent out rooms for short terms. He's going to rent one for Mama."

"I can't believe Mama has to live with

strangers. There should be a special hotel run by the hospital so that families can stay together."

"It's the way things are, for now," Adel said, picking up her plate of barely eaten food.

I picked up mine and followed her into the kitchen. I'd completely lost my appetite, and for once I couldn't blame it on my sister's cooking.

On Saturday morning, before we left for Emory, I took an enormous vase out into the yard and cut flowers from the gardens. I filled the vase with sprays of pink and purple crepe myrtle blossoms, autumn roses, hydrangeas, the last of the summer's black-eyed Susans and the first of the fall mums.

I climbed into the backseat holding the huge arrangement, and Papa asked, "Did you leave anything *in* the yard, honey?"

"I just want Mama to enjoy her gardens," I said. "Until she can come see them again for herself."

"The flowers are fine," Papa said. "I'm sure she'll be pleased."

She was. When I walked into the room with the vase, her whole face lit up. She hugged us all, begged us for news from home. Adel chattered about household things and I told her about school; the upcoming high school football game against Redford, a rival of Conners for years; and the arrival of Jason and J.T.'s lack of consideration toward him.

"I've met Jason," Mama said. "Jim and Carole stopped by on their way home from the airport and he was with them. He seemed like an unhappy young man, so I hope you'll be kind to him, Darcy. I know what it feels like to be far away from home. I'm sure he's missing all things familiar."

"Do you know if he plays football?" I asked out of the blue.

"No, I don't know. Why do you ask?"

"No reason," I said.

Mama was dressed in regular clothes, but she looked pale and thinner than when I'd last seen her. I could tell she was having trouble moving her arm, wrapped in an elastic sleeve. She held a small rubber ball that she kept squeezing. "The sleeve keeps the swelling down, and the ball squeezing is an exercise to help me get my strength in my arm back," she said, seeing me staring. "I still have a drainage tube in place."

It had to have been hidden beneath her clothes because I couldn't see anything. "I sure wish you were coming home, Mama," I said.

"Me too. But I can't." She forced a quick smile. "They tell me that the radiation makes a person dog-tired, and that the chemo makes a person dog-sick, so it's better I stay here anyway."

"And then it'll all be over? You'll be well and won't have to come back here again?"

"I'll have to come in for regular blood tests."

In my mind, I'd figured that over meant over, but with cancer it must not mean that at all.

"All your friends are asking about you," Adel said. "I don't know what to tell them."

Mama sighed. "I guess I can't keep this a secret. Carole's already told the Women's Prayer Fellowship, so if you don't want to answer questions, tell people to call Carole."

I felt better knowing that the First Baptist prayer warriors were storming heaven on Mama's behalf. God would have to listen to them!

"You know what?" Papa interjected. "I'm getting a wheelchair from the nurses' station and we're taking your mother out for a walk around the grounds. It's a beautiful day and getting outside will cheer us all up."

So that's what we did. Papa pushed Mama, and Adel and I walked on either side. Somewhere someone was burning leaves, because the October air smelled faintly of smoke. Trees were taking on the colors of autumn and the sky was a brilliant shade of blue shot through with sunlight.

Mama tipped back her head and opened her arms wide toward the sky. "Fall is surely my favorite time of year," she said. "Next to spring. Nothing's better than the smell of fresh earth, or prettier than flowers and trees beginning to bloom."

"By spring this will all be over," Papa said. "You'll be digging up the beds and putting in flowers."

Mama looked over at me. "Darcy, the hostas will need cutting down and the bulbs should be brought out of the cellar for planting."

"I'll do it, Mama," I said.

"Nothing's going to stop my gardens from blooming in the spring. Not even cancer."

We all agreed. Our mama had a fighting spirit, and nothing brought it out quicker than the fear of her gardens going fallow.


We started home in the late afternoon, after a tearful goodbye. I was in a funk in the backseat and didn't notice for a long time that Papa was driving a different route home. A fence ran along the road we were traveling. Signs read Property of the United States Army, and then all at once a booth with a wooden guardrail loomed in front of us. A uniformed man wearing an MP armband stepped out. Papa stopped and gave his name, and the MP checked his name off a list on the clipboard he held, put a card that read Visitor's Pass under our windshield wiper and waved us through the gate.

I couldn't keep silent any longer. "Where are we going?"

"I'm meeting Barry," Adel said.

I couldn't figure when she'd made those arrangements with Papa. "Why didn't you tell me?" I asked.

"I didn't think I had to clear it with you," she answered.

"It would have been nice to know," I said huffily.

"Calm down, ladies," Papa said. "Let's not start a war right here on Georgia soil."

Papa drove along neat, well-ordered streets, and I looked out onto open fields with rows of wooden barracks and low metal buildings.

"There it is," Adel said, pointing at a free-standing white building with a sign reading Enlisted Men's Club.

Papa slowed, and the car had barely stopped rolling when Adel jumped out and ran to a man dressed in uniform standing on the steps. He took both her hands and pulled her close.

Papa parked the car and we walked over to the two of them. When Adel turned, I saw that her cheeks were pink and her eyes glowing. "Papa, Darcy, I want you to meet Barry Sorenson."

"Barry Sorenson, Specialist Fourth Class, Electronics," the man said. He saluted, then shook Papa's hand. He turned to me. "And I see that beauty runs in the family."

I felt my face turning pink. Barry Sorenson

was gorgeous. Tall, trim, black hair in a buzz cut and dark blue eyes—plus, he could have stopped a charging bull with his smile.

"Pleased to meet you, son," Papa said. "Adel's told me many things about you."

*When?* I wanted to know but didn't dare ask. *She's never said a thing to me!*

"And she's told me about you and her mother too, sir," Barry said. "Thank you for bringing her all the way out here today."

Barry put his arm around Adel's waist. They looked into each other's eyes and I knew beyond a shadow of a doubt that he was head over heels in love with my sister. But then, wasn't every man who ever laid eyes on her?

# Six

Papa said, "Adel tells me you're in special training."

"Yes, sir. I'm attached to a Lockheed training and missile control project, but once that's done I belong to the army one hundred percent. I don't get passes off the base very often, so I appreciate your making this trip to bring her to me. I know these are difficult times, with your wife's illness and all."

The way he said the words "bring her to me" sounded intimate and made a shiver run up my spine. Adel sure could pick winners.

"Yes, Joy's illness is hard on me and the girls, but she wants us to go on with regular life, so that's what we're doing," Papa said. "She's a fine, brave woman."

Adel said, "Want to get a cola before you get back on the road, Papa?"

"All right." Papa put his hand on my shoulder. "How about you, Darcy? Care to wet your whistle?"

Wild horses couldn't have dragged me away from the opportunity.

We walked to a stand that sold sodas, candy and snack items, bought what we wanted and sat together at a nearby picnic table. Papa said, "Adel tells me you hail from New York City."

"I was born upstate," Barry said. "My parents moved to the city when I was ten. My father's a cop and Mom works for an insurance company. I have an older brother. He served in Nam with the marines in the late sixties."

Another shiver shot through me as I recalled video of the war I'd seen on TV. "Is he okay?" I blurted out, without thinking. They stared at me and I blushed, realizing that I was once again being nosey. "I'm—um—studying Vietnam in school," I explained, hoping to smooth over the awkward moment. "All I know about Vietnam is what I read in newspapers, or see on TV, which isn't so much anymore. I've never talked to anyone who's been there firsthand."

"Kyle's home in one piece," Barry said, his eyes serious. "I can't say he's okay, though. He's in and out of the VA hospital."

"Why's that?"

Adel flashed me a look that said *Would you hush up?* and slipped her hand into Barry's.

Papa said, "Perhaps this isn't the appropriate time to talk about this, Darcy."

Barry said, "It's all right. America still has personnel over there, but people forget because it's not in the news as much as it once was. As for my brother, he was never wounded in the flesh, just in his psyche. He suffers from what doctors call post-traumatic stress. The things he went through during his combat were so bad that his mind can't let go of them. He's had a lot of trouble fitting back into the normal world."

I'd never heard of such a thing.

Papa said, "In World War Two, it was called combat fatigue or shell shock."

"Were you in World War Two, sir?"

Papa shook his head. "By the time I was eighteen and old enough to sign up, the war was over. In those days, we counted it a privilege to fight for our country. I missed Korea because I had family obligations and Vietnam because I was too old. I admire men who serve our nation, though."

Papa had been born in 1929 and he and Mama married in 1954. Adel came along in 1955 and me in 1960. My father had seen three wars thus far in his lifetime but hadn't fought in any of them, and he sounded sorry about it.

Papa stood. "We'd better get on the road, Darcy."

I gave Adel a questioning look, and she said, "Sandy's driving over this evening and I'll come home with her. For now, Barry and I will just keep each other company." She gave him a flirtatious smile and he grinned.

Barry shook Papa's hand. "I'll take good care of her, sir."

"You're the one who'll need looking after, son. Southern women are not to be trifled with. They look delicate as lace, but they've got rods of steel running through them," Papa joked good-naturedly.

Adel said, "Oh, Papa, stop it . . . you'll scare him off."

"Not likely," Barry said.

On the drive home, I was quiet, mulling over what I'd seen and heard that day. After a long time, I said, "Adel and Barry seem to really like each other."

"Yes, they do."

"What's Mama think?"

"She wants Adel to be happy, and if Barry makes her happy . . ." He didn't finish the sentence, but he didn't have to.

"I miss Mama," I said. "We'll be going a long time without her. And an extra-long time having to eat Adel's cooking."

"We surely will," Papa said, sounding wistful.

We looked at each other, then burst out laughing. Evidently, we both held the same opinion of Adel's kitchen skills.

Papa said, "I was thinking that maybe we should start having Sunday dinner down at the Southern Grille." He named the single restaurant in Conners other than the Woolworth soda counter and the brand-new Kentucky Fried Chicken fast-food store.

"Sounds like a reasonable idea," I told him. "Potluck supper at church on Wednesday night, Sunday afternoon in a restaurant." Two out of seven meals Adel wasn't cooking. "I'll bet Friday night is good for takeout from Kentucky Fried," I ventured.

"Don't push it, Darcy," Papa said. "The girl needs to practice sometime."

On Friday night, Conners' football team played Redford, one of our toughest rivals, at the Redford field. Russell still hadn't taken the kind of notice of Becky Sue that would result in his asking her on a date, so we were with each other, as usual. Becky's dad drove us to the game and stayed, but he sat high up in the bleachers with other Conners parents and alumni, which left Becky Sue and me to sandwich ourselves between our classmates in the lower seats.

The night had turned chilly, so we were bundled up and had an old quilt thrown across our laps. Both bands were playing, and people in both sets of bleachers were cheering. Rebel flags waved, and since it was Redford's homecoming, we were watching their queen and her court sashay around the field.

"Who do you think will be elected queen at our school?" Becky yelled above the noise of the crowd.

"Neither one of us," I shouted back.

As the court passed in front of our stands, some senior boys yelled out a few rude remarks and received threatening looks from the Redford court in return. I remembered when Adel had been queen and had ridden around our high school field in Tom Chapman's red convertible. She had looked beautiful perched atop the backseat, wearing a sparkling tiara and holding a scepter just like a real queen. Fleetingly, I wondered if any boy would ever look at me the way Barry had looked at Adel, a memory I could not get out of my mind. I'd told Becky Sue that he'd looked at her ". . . like she'd been ice cream, and him starving for it."

Becky Sue poked me in the ribs. "Look, there's Jason."

My heart did a stutter-step at the sight of him. He stood at the side of the field, elbows braced on the top of the four-foot chain-link fence. He wore the old leather jacket and a black knit ski hat.

"Looks like he's all alone. Maybe we should ask him to sit with us." The words were out before I could stop them.

Becky gave me a quizzical look. "Why would we do that?"

"Just being friendly. Like Pastor Jim asked." I knew my face was turning red and the last thing I wanted was for Becky Sue to start giving me the third degree.

Fortunately, our football team ran out onto the field and the stands went wild with cheering. Even I had to admit that the team appeared formidable. Especially J.T. He looked as big as a barn dressed out in pads and helmet. The opposition came onto the field, the captains met in the middle and the referee flipped a coin. It went our way and our team elected to kick off. The announcer on the PA system asked for silence while a minister said a prayer, which I figured Redford needed more than us; then the band played the national anthem and the whistle blew to start the game. All the while, I couldn't help noticing that J.T. kept twitching and tugging at his uniform britches. I guessed even guys like him got nervous before a big game.

The teams got into formation on the field, but just as the referee put the whistle in his mouth, the strangest thing happened. J.T. gave a yelp, stood straight up and commenced to dancing and whooping like a wild man, all the while grabbing at his private parts. For a stunned second, no one moved; then laughter erupted from both sets of bleachers, followed by catcalls.

"You got hot pants, J.T.?" someone shouted.

"Hey, J.T., hands off the family jewels!" called another.

Coach rushed out onto the field and practically had to subdue J.T. with a headlock. Finally, he got him off the field and pointed toward the locker room, but by then all was in chaos. The teams had started slugging it out, and students poured out of the stands to join the melee. Both bands started marching and playing in an attempt to drown out the shouting, all the while bumping into each other. Becky and I had the good sense to sit tight. Someone could get hurt in the confusion, and we didn't want it to be either of us.

My view became obscured by people running past. Parents shouted for somebody to get the police. I couldn't stop laughing, remembering the sight of J.T.'s impromptu war dance. *Whatever in the world had happened?* I turned in time to see Jason push away from the fence and cut through the crowds, going against the surge of bodies like a fish swimming upstream. He looked up, and for a brief moment our gazes locked. His eyes were cool, his expression satisfied. He nodded at me, shoved his hands into the pockets of his jacket and disappeared into the parking lot. I watched him go, my brain on fire with curiosity, my heart aflame from the contact.

The game wasn't played that night and it took every cop in Redford and two Georgia state troopers to disperse the crowd. The story made the eleven o'clock news in both cities. The Saturday sports section alluded to a "vicious, unsportsmanlike prank perpetrated on J. T. Rucker, defensive center for the Conners Rebels." And, "Inquiries are being made by police and school officials alike. When the culprit is apprehended, he will be punished."

I read the story several times, all the while chuckling at the memory of J.T. whooping and hollering and grabbing himself on the field with half the county watching. Of course, I knew that no one at school would dare tease him about it unless they had a death wish. Still, it was payback for the many times over the years that J.T. had bullied kids who couldn't fight back.

On Monday, our principal, Mr. Hagan, came on the PA and told the whole school that what had happened at the game wasn't funny and that if anyone knew anything, blah, blah, blah. I tuned him out midway through his speech. By lunchtime it was all over school that the "prankster" had somehow managed to put itching powder on J.T.'s jockstrap, thus causing his odd behavior and war dance. Seems like it left burned patches on his delicate skin too. "A shame," I said to Becky Sue while keeping a straight face.

"A *crying* shame," she said in agreement.

My life fell into a pattern for the time that Mama was away receiving cancer treatments. Weekdays, Adel and Papa went to work and I went to school. On Saturdays we'd drive to Atlanta and visit with Mama. Papa had found her a nice private room with an elderly widow two blocks from the hospital, where Mama went daily.

After our Saturday visits with Mama, Papa would drive Adel to the base, where Barry would meet her. Papa and I would come on home and Adel would ride home later at night with her friend Sandy, who also had a soldier beau at the base. On Sundays we'd go to church, then out to eat at the Southern Grille. Sunday nights, I'd attend teen group with Becky. Then it would be Monday, and the cycle would start all over.

After school I worked in the gardens, digging up annuals, planting bulbs and deadheading spent blossoms from plants getting ready to cozy down for the winter. I also did my homework, including research for my special project. After talking to

Barry, world events had a whole lot more meaning for me. The Irish Republican Army was blowing up buildings in Great Britain, the Palestine Liberation Organization was formally recognized, and fighting continued in Vietnam and also its neighbor Cambodia. Seemed to me like the whole world was at war.

In the middle of October, Pastor Jim reminded us about the not-to-be-missed annual hayride.

"Our group's so large that we're getting two trucks of hay this year," the pastor announced. "Middle-schoolers in one, high-schoolers in the other. We'll go along the Simmons property to their south field. It's not planted this year and they've kindly said we can build a bonfire and raise our voices to praise the Lord.

"And," Pastor Jim added, "I expect all of you to come."

He looked straight at Jason when he said that, and my pulse raced, for I spent much of my free time daydreaming about Jason. He seemed mysterious to me, not needing or wanting anybody's company or approval. If I saw him in the halls, my heartbeat went crazy and my breath felt knocked out of me. My reactions appalled me—hadn't I teased Becky Sue about the silliness of such things? And yet now it was happening to me and there wasn't a soul I'd dare tell. I decided that my feelings toward Jason were part of a conspiracy of nature to mess up teenagers' minds. Trouble was, I couldn't figure out *why*. What was the point in making us feel like we were going crazy? All I wanted was the safety of my old world. Instead, I was being dragged into this new one, where the water was deep and dark. And I didn't know if I'd be able to swim.

# Seven

~~~ ~~~

"This one, or this one?" I asked Becky Sue, holding up two pullover sweaters for her inspection.

We were in my room and she was helping me decide what to wear for the hayride on Saturday night.

"It gets awful hot around that bonfire," Becky Sue said.

The weather didn't turn really cold in our part of Georgia until near Thanksgiving, but I liked wearing loose-fitting sweaters because they hid my skinny body and flat chest. "Good point," I said. "I'll wear a long-sleeved shirt under the sweater, and if I'm burning up, I can strip."

"That will impress the church crowd."

"You know what I mean." I pawed through my closet, looking for my favorite denim shirt.

"Why are you trying so hard?" Becky asked. "It's just the hayride. It's not like we've never gone before."

That was true. But before, we'd just been kids and Jason hadn't been on my mind morning, noon and night. I turned back to my closet. If Becky suspected for one second that I wanted to look good for Jason, I'd never live it down. "Are you saying you're not planning what you're going to wear?"

"Why? Russell won't be there."

Russell's family attended the Second Baptist Church, so he wouldn't be coming to our church's activity. "You could ask him," I suggested.

"Are you crazy? Then he'll know I like him."

"Well, he doesn't seem to be catching on any other way."

Becky Sue flopped backward dramatically. "Don't you know anything about snagging a guy? I want *him* to figure out that he likes *me*. I can't go throwing myself at him. He'll think I'm desperate."

"Aren't you?" Her logic escaped me.

She threw a bed pillow at me. "You just wait until you have the hots for some boy, then we'll see how you go about making him notice you."

I picked up the pillow. "Well, if I ever do, what advice would you give me?"

"I'd tell you to ask your sister. If her soldier

boyfriend is as good-looking as you say he is, then she sure knows more about catching boys than I do." Becky boosted herself up on her elbows. "You sure you'll be back in time for the hayride on Saturday?"

"Papa says we'll be home by six." Dropping Adel off at the army base was taking less time because Barry met us at the guard gate.

"Come straight to my house and Mom will run us up to the church together."

I agreed readily, because I really didn't want to show up alone. "You never did tell me which sweater you liked best on me."

Becky Sue pursed her lips, pondering the choices. "The blue one," she finally said. "It matches your eyes, which, by the way, are your best feature."

I held the blue sweater under my chin and checked out my reflection in the mirror over my dresser. The color did complement my eyes. I wondered if Jason had ever noticed the color of my eyes. Suddenly I remembered that by the time he'd see me on Saturday night, it would be dark. He wouldn't be able to *see* the color of my eyes.

The house where Mama rented a room had been built in the 1930s and was located on a quiet tree-lined street. I thought the place depressing but kept my opinion to myself. Mama's room held a bed and a dresser, an overstuffed chair and a braided rug. There was a white-tiled bathroom across the short hallway, and Mama had free use of the living room, where the furniture lay wrapped in slipcovers and the windows were masked by heavy floral-print drapes. Pictures of people none of us knew lined the end tables. There was an old black-and-white TV set in one corner, with rabbit ears wrapped in aluminum foil for better reception.

When we came to visit, Papa toted in chairs from the kitchen so that we'd all have a place to sit. If the weather was pretty and Mama was feeling up to it, we'd sit out on the old porch.

I was hoping that Mama's treatments were doing her a powerful lot of good on the inside, because they weren't doing her any favors on the outside. She looked pale and thin, and she had taken to wearing a bandana because her once shiny auburn hair was falling out in clumps. Her arms were bruised from the IVs. Dark circles under her eyes seemed to grow deeper each week. We never asked how she was feeling, because any fool with half a brain could tell she hurt.

That Saturday of the hayride, I was alone with Mama at the house because Papa and Adel had gone to the store to buy her ice cream and some other things she needed. "The chemo gives me powerful odd cravings, when I can keep food down," she'd told them. "And ice cream helps the sores inside my mouth feel better."

So we were together alone for the first time since before she'd come to the hospital. She was sitting up in the bed. The room felt stuffy, but she had said she was cold, so I didn't dare open the window.

"How have you been, Darcy?" she asked me.

Tears welled up in my eyes. "I miss you, Mama. I miss coming home from school and you being there. I miss the way things used to be."

She took my hand and urged me onto the bed beside her. She wrapped her arms around me and let me cry. "I miss you too. I want to come home so much. But I can't just yet. I have to get better. Licking cancer is a hard thing to do."

I pulled away. "But you will, Mama. Please say you will."

She smoothed my forehead. "Course I will. Don't you worry about that. Now tell me something about school. You're making good grades, aren't you?"

I nodded, but my mind turned to other things. "Mama, how does someone know if she's in love?"

"Why are you asking?"

"No reason." I was suddenly embarrassed over my dumb question. Then inspiration struck. "I see Adel and Barry, and she's had lots of boyfriends, but this time it seems different. Why does a person get all nervous and jittery every time she gets around the person she likes? I mean, is it normal for your stomach to get tied up in knots? Becky Sue says that's what happens to her all the time when she likes somebody special."

"Well, Becky Sue should know. She's been in love—let's see—how many times? Six? Ten?"

I smiled and laid my head on Mama's shoulder. "A lot."

"Love is a mystery. And there's no denying the fireworks part—those feelings of thinking your heart's going to bang right out of your chest whenever you see that special someone." Mama understood just what I was talking about. "Chemistry and hormones come into play for sure," she continued. "But love can't be discerned by those things alone."

"But how do you *know*?"

"I would say that a sign of true love is that it happens slowly, like a friendship. It will be respectful and kind, and it will have a short memory for hurtful times between the couple. Love is like the plants in our gardens. It has to be watered and nurtured and kept safe from frost and heat. But when it blooms—ah, my dear daughter—when it blooms, there is no fragrance sweeter."

*Love is sweet.* What I felt when I was around

Jason was not sweet contentment. It was edgy and unsettling. "I'll stick with the plants, because love sounds like a lot of bother to me," I said.

"Love will find you one day, Darcy. And it won't be a bother." I could hear the smile in her voice.

"If you say so, Mama."

I stayed in my mother's arms until she drifted off to sleep.

I arrived at Becky's house, nervous but excited about the hayride and seeing Jason. Her mother opened the door and dropped a bomb on me. "Darcy, she's not going."

"What? B-but why?" Becky *had* to go. We always went to these things together.

"She's not feeling well."

I took the stairs two at a time and burst into Becky's bedroom. Becky Sue lay on her bed, a hot-water bottle pressed over her lower abdomen. "You have to go without me," she moaned. "I have the curse."

I stared at her. Why had Mother Nature visited her today, of all days? "But you've got to come," I said. "Did you take aspirin?"

"All afternoon," Becky said. "I'm still hurting."

Being the late bloomer I was, I had not had the problems with my period that Becky had.

She'd started her monthly cycle when she was twelve. I was almost fourteen before mine decided to drop in on me. I had even lied when I was just turning thirteen, saying I had "it" when I didn't because I felt like such a freak over not having it. Once I did get it, I wished it had not befallen me. I found "it" a terrible inconvenience. Our gym teacher made girls sit out sports when they were having their periods, which I hated because I loved sports and resented not playing when I felt perfectly fine. Yet, at the moment, I saw that Becky Sue did not feel fine and jumping on her about missing the hayride wasn't going to change anything. If I was going to the hayride, I would have to go alone.

"This stinks," I said.

"True," Becky moaned. "But I'm telling you, I can't move. You go on and have fun and tell me all about it."

For a moment I thought about not going; then I remembered Jason and wrestled with my two options: being without my best friend all evening, or not seeing the one—and only—boy who had ever made my pulse flutter. My internal wrestling match was short-lived. "You feel better," I said to Becky Sue. I shut the door and left her to her misery.

Becky's mother ran me up to the church parking lot and told me to have a "good enough time for Becky too." I got out of her car and walked over to the crowd of kids waiting to pile onto the two hay wagons once Pastor Jim gave the word. The "wagons" really were large flatbed trucks heaped with fresh straw. Trucks were used because we'd have to drive to the field for the bonfire on back country roads. The ride would take about forty minutes. Slatted sides and a tailgate kept us all fenced in safely, and because the trucks were so big, there was plenty of room.

The sixth graders were chasing each other and stuffing handfuls of straw down each other's clothes. *Babies!* I strolled over to the other wagon, the one for the high-schoolers, and with alarm saw that I was the only ninth-grade girl who had come. The older girls looked me over.

"Where's your shadow?" Donna McGowen asked, not very kindly.

"I thought you two were Siamese twins," her friend Laverne added, making the group of girls giggle.

"Good one," Donna said to Laverne.

I bit my tongue, figuring I needed to be respectful because we were on church property. "Not that you care, but Becky's sick," I told them.

"What a shame." J.T. and three of his thug friends materialized from the far side of the wagon. He slung his arm over Donna's shoulder. "Now you really are dateless."

The whole group of them roared. Fortunately, Pastor Jim blew a whistle before I could say something I might regret.

"All aboard," he called out.

I scrambled on quickly, knowing I didn't want to crawl past J.T. and his friends if they boarded first. I'd hoped that Carole might go with us, but through the slats, I saw her on the other wagon. I walked to the front of the truck and sat down in the rough straw, wedging myself into the corner. With a start, I saw that Jason was directly across from me, under the window of the truck's cab. I'd been so involved with Donna and J.T. that I'd forgotten to look for him. I realized that he'd been up there the whole time and had witnessed my being teased.

Just seeing him made my knees go weak. He was nimbly rolling a stick from finger to finger and took no notice of me. The truck filled amid squeals of "Help me up, J.T." And "You're so strong, J.T." And "Move over closer, Donna, and keep the chill off." It was enough to make a person nauseous.

I looked up. The night sky was filled with a full moon that shone as bright as a light. A lover's moon, we called it in Georgia. It only made me feel worse. I wished I hadn't come.

# Eight

The trucks set off. Someone had brought a transistor radio, and Olivia Newton-John started singing her hit song "I Honestly Love You." Her beautiful voice and the touching words of the song filled the night. I listened as she sang "I love you; I honestly love you," and I felt my throat tighten as an ache filled me. I didn't love anyone. Not in the way she was singing about.

I saw J.T. nuzzling Donna's neck and wished Pastor Jim was riding in the back instead of inside the cab. Couldn't he have guessed that J.T. was going to try to put the moves on his girlfriend? I snuck sidelong glances at the others. Everybody seemed paired off. Except for me.

The music kept playing. I wanted to clap my hands over my ears. Tears swam in my eyes. I was embarrassing myself over a silly song and feelings

I couldn't seem to turn off. I blinked hard to stop a tear from moving down my cheek. When I turned my head, I saw that Jason was looking straight at me. I was mortified. "Dust in my eyes," I said, hoping he believed me. "I forgot I'm allergic to straw."

He looked away, but I could not forget the feel of his eyes on me. It had been as if he could see inside me. I felt undressed, and I crossed my arms over my chest and hunkered down into the straw. At last the song ended and the radio played something more upbeat. I got mad at Becky Sue for getting her period and not coming. And mad at myself for coming anyway.

The ride seemed interminable, but finally the truck turned into a large open field and stopped in the center, where a huge pile of wood had already been laid for the bonfire. Logs for us to sit on had been placed around the perimeter of the pile. A table, holding stacks of hot dogs and buns and bags of marshmallows, stood to one side. Three ice chests held cold drinks. J.T. leaned over one, rummaged and came up with a bottle of orange soda. "What, no beer?" he asked, making kids laugh.

"Cool it, J.T.," Pastor Jim admonished.

Carole came to me and asked about Mama. "She doesn't look real good," I said.

"Chemo is difficult," Carole said, "but I'm sure

her doctors are doing what's best for her." She handed me a paper plate and a raw hot dog. "Darcy, your mother has so many friends who want to do something for her."

I shrugged. "There's nothing anybody can do."

"We can help her family."

"How so?"

"Her friends can take turns bringing over suppers for as long as she's in Atlanta. I'll organize a list of her church family and garden club ladies, if that's all right. I know Adel's cooking for your family, but—"

"That would be great," I said before she could even finish her sentence.

"Your mother's been so good to me, and I'd love to help your family while she's going through this."

Carole moved off and I stared down at the plate I held. The hot dog looked unappetizing. Still, the fire had been lit and kids were roasting their dinners on sticks they'd found in the field. I went off in search of one for myself.

I'd gotten a late start in the stick search. The ones closer to the fire had already been claimed. I was glad of the moonlight as I looked over the ground, walking farther into the field. I circled around a clump of live oak trees, and a voice asked, "Who's there?"

Startled, I jumped backward and dropped my plate.

The red glow of a cigarette preceded Jason from the other side of a tree. "Oh, it's you," he said.

"You scared me to death," I whispered fiercely. My heart was pounding, and not just from fright. "What are you doing over here? And—are you smoking?"

He pulled the cigarette from his mouth and offered it to me. "Want a drag?"

I'd never had such a long conversation with him, and suddenly he was inviting me to smoke with him. If I took the cigarette, would he think I was mature and sophisticated? I almost reached for it. "Uh—no thanks. I don't smoke," I finally said, picturing myself having a coughing fit in front of him. That was what had happened the one time Becky and I had tried smoking.

He took a long drag, dropped the butt and ground it into the dirt with the toe of his boot. "Good. Girls who smoke look trashy."

I stood feeling self-conscious as the acrid smell of the cigarette dissipated into the cool night air. I caught the subtle scent of his leather jacket and cinnamon as he popped a breath mint into his mouth. "You looking for a stick to roast a hot dog?" I asked. I had no experience talking to boys. Not to boys who made my heart beat faster and my knees wobbly.

"I came because Carole and Jim made me come," Jason said. "As you might have figured out, I don't like being here. And I don't just mean at this hayride."

I knew. "I reckon Conners is a big letdown after living in Chicago."

"I promised Carole I'd finish high school."

"Is that why you're staying?"

"That's the only reason."

I thought of how J.T. and his jock friends had treated Jason from the minute he'd arrived. "You know, we're not all like J.T.," I said.

"People give him a lot of respect. Why is that?"

I remembered Mama's philosophy: If you can't say something nice about someone, don't say anything at all. "Because he plays football. But everybody knows he's a bully," I said, ignoring Mama's maxim. "And he always has been. Although I guess it's not his fault he was born big. But his meanness has been carefully cultivated."

Jason laughed. "You have colorful ways of putting things."

I felt my cheeks going hot and I was glad for the darkness under the trees. "Well, not everybody thinks J.T. is as cool as he thinks he is," I said. "I've known him all my life. He had a terrible crush on my older sister, Adel, but she didn't pay him one bit of attention. I always respected Adel for that. They were two years apart anyway, so J.T. never really had a chance with her." I realized that I was babbling about things Jason wasn't one bit interested in and clamped my lips together before I made a bigger fool of myself.

In the silence, I heard Pastor Jim playing his guitar across the field and voices singing gospel songs. "I guess I'd better get back."

Jason reached out and caught my arm. "Can I ask you something?"

My heart started thudding and his hand made my skin feel warm beneath the layers of clothing I wore. "Course," I answered.

"What's important to J.T.?"

The question caught me by surprise and for a minute stymied me. "I—um—gee—I guess football is most important to him," I said.

"What other things?"

"Well, he drives his uncle's old battered pickup, which is more like a battering ram than a real car, so that's not important. And books aren't important because reading and writing are just excuses he uses to play football." I thought for a minute. "I reckon Donna, his girlfriend, is his current best interest. Though I surely don't know why. Oh, she's pretty and all, but thoughtfulness and kindness are not her strong suits, if you get my meaning. But how can you not get my meaning? I'm sorry, that's not very charitable of me to say those things about her—"

"It's okay. Slow down. You're making me dizzy."

My face felt hot again. "Sorry." I knew I'd said too much and that I should leave, but I didn't want to. We stood in the darkness listening to the music.

"Carole really likes your mother," Jason said after a time.

"Mama likes Carole too," I said.

"Your mother's sick, isn't she?"

"She has cancer, but she's getting treatments, so I figure she'll be one hundred percent real soon." I felt odd discussing my mother with him, then remembered that they'd met when he'd first arrived.

He reached into a pocket and pulled out a pack of cigarettes, put one between his lips and lit up. "You better go on before you're missed."

I took a step, feeling like a little kid being sent out of a room. "What about you? Won't they start looking around and see that you're not there?"

"I'll come after I finish this smoke."

I started to go.

"Darcy." The way he said my name sent a shiver up my spine. "Thanks for talking to me."

"Anytime," I said, meaning it with all my heart.

"Don't let them make you cry," he added.

I wanted him to know that he had made a wrong assumption. "It was the song," I said. "I don't know why it affected me, but it did."

"It's a pretty song," he said. "I like it too."

I walked off, feeling light as a feather, the memory of his voice going over me like water over dry ground.

On Sunday after Papa, Adel and I ate downtown, I went to Becky's and told her about the hayride. I didn't tell her everything exactly as it happened. I just said that I'd had my first bona fide talk with Jason and that he seemed lonely. I dwelled on Donna and J.T. and their rudeness and got total sympathy from Becky.

On Halloween, she came to my house and helped pass out candy to the kids who came trick-or-treating. Every little ghost and goblin made me remember all the times I'd gone in the costumes Mama made for me. Whatever I told her I longed to be, she somehow managed to create it. I'd been an Indian princess, a fairy queen and Tony the Tiger. My last year of dressing up I'd gone as Marcia Brady, complete with wig. Mama let me eat all my candy too. She didn't parcel it out the way

Becky's mother did. No, I ate it until I got sick of it.

Early the next morning, Papa woke me from a sound sleep with a roar. "Darcy Quinlin, come down here this minute!"

I staggered downstairs, half asleep, heart pounding. He stood in the doorway, looking livid. "What's wrong?" I asked.

He pushed open the front door and I went out on the porch and gasped. Our front lawn was a sea of white. Someone had toilet-papered our trees, bushes and car. Morning dampness had caused the paper to shred and sag. "I don't know which one of your hoodlum friends did this, but you're going to clean up every last dollop, *now*. Is that clear?"

"B-but I—I'll be late for school."

"Clean it up!" He slammed the screen door and retreated into the house.

Papa was boiling mad, but so was I. Whoever had done this knew I would get into trouble. And naturally, I could think of only one person who would do such a childish, stupid prank. J.T. I was as certain of it as I was of my name.

I gritted my teeth, found a plastic lawn bag and began the long, tedious task of raking up the soggy toilet paper. "I'll get even with you someday, J.T.," I muttered as I worked. I didn't know how or when, but I would. I surely would.

# Nine
## *November*

It became harder to go to Atlanta every Saturday. Not because I didn't want to see Mama—I did. But because I could hardly stand to see what the chemo was doing to her. Her hair was gone, even her eyebrows and eyelashes. "Better tell Marcia I won't be needing that weekly appointment at her salon," Mama would say in an effort to make light of her loss.

She grew thinner. "Now I can eat all the chocolate I want," she'd tell us. She grew weaker. "I think I'll just sit here in bed and visit with you today, if you don't mind." She grew more tired. "Let me just doze a minute, all right? Now, don't leave. I want to visit more right after a little catnap."

I cried every week on the way home. "Seems to me the chemotherapy is killing her," I'd wail from the backseat.

"Now you hush," Adel would hiss. "Sure it's bad, but it's killing the cancer too."

Papa didn't say much of anything. He looked grim and sad and lost without Mama.

Carole and some of the church ladies drove over on Mondays to visit Mama. And casseroles, fried chicken, roasts and other yummy Southern cooking showed up at our house every evening like clockwork. We were all grateful. Not only because the food was good, but because we were all worn down from the strain of holding things together. It wasn't just that we missed Mama, but her absence had left a hole in our family and we didn't know how to realign ourselves to fill in the empty space.

Papa stayed late at the bank working most nights. After work, Adel shut herself in her room and wrote long letters to Barry and talked on the phone to Sandy. I buried myself in my schoolwork. The college-prep courses were tougher than other schoolwork I'd done over the years, so I doubled my efforts on every assignment, telling myself that Mama would be proud if she knew how hard I was trying.

We were sitting on the porch of the little house, visiting Mama, when Adel said, "I want to ask Barry to come for Thanksgiving. His commander is offering three-day passes and I want to invite him to stay with us. He can't get to New

York and back, and I'd hate for him to spend the holiday stuck at the base."

"I don't know—" Papa started.

Mama interrupted. "Why, that's a wonderful idea. Poor boy's so far away from home. He should be with a family."

"I'll cook, Papa," Adel said quickly. "I know all of Mama's recipes."

Papa and I exchanged glances, and I knew we were thinking the same thing about Adel's cooking and wanting Barry to enjoy the meal and still be fond of Adel. "Um—I'll help," I said.

"I think the girls should do it," Mama said.

"What about Barry staying over?" Adel asked. "That way we can have two whole days with each other."

"He'll need a place to sleep," Papa said. "The back porch is too cold this time of year. Your mother would fret herself silly if we didn't offer him a proper room."

Mama agreed.

"Barry can have my room. I'll sleep on the living room sofa," Adel said.

I knew what I had to do to save the day. I said, "Barry can have my room and I'll sleep on a cot in Adel's room. My bathroom is right across the hall, and Adel and I can share hers."

All eyes turned to me.

"That's hospitable of you, Darcy," Mama said.

"I appreciate your offer," Adel said. She looked relieved and even grateful.

I felt like a hero.

I was in the cafeteria, eating a late lunch by myself. I had been excused from my regular lunch period because I'd been in speech class practicing for an upcoming debate, so I was still eating when the juniors and seniors came in.

The football team had a special table set aside where they ate together every day. The team was into state playoffs—they'd won our district—and everyone in Conners was cutting them a lot of slack. As if they needed it. They already behaved like they were royalty, which they weren't, but the newspaper kept them on the front page and everywhere they went people bowed and scraped. I never understood why football got more attention than high grades, but it did.

Fortunately, J.T.'s back was to me. I shoveled my food, swallowing without tasting. I wanted out of there before he took notice of me. I was almost finished when I looked up to see Jason coming out of the line. He started toward a table by the windows. Unfortunately, he had to pass the football table to get there. That was when I saw J.T.'s foot snake out into Jason's path. Jason didn't see it.

My breath caught. I stood up and yelled,

"Jason, watch out!" But my warning came too late.

Jason went down and his tray clattered to the floor, scattering its contents every which way. The voices in the cafeteria stopped humming and every head turned to see what had happened.

"Whoops," J.T. said, leaning back in his chair. "Didn't see you coming, man."

I couldn't see his expression, but I knew it wasn't one bit sorry looking.

Jason got back on his feet. His jeans were smeared with vanilla pudding and his hands sopping with soup. He slung off the wetness, making sure some of it hit J.T. "You did that on purpose," Jason said. His voice was low, his face pale as milk.

"Didn't either. Did I, guys?" J.T. looked to his friends, who all shook their heads.

Jason rested his palms on the edge of the table and leaned into J.T.'s face. "Know what your problem is, J.T.? You think everybody's afraid of you. Well, I'm not." Jason's gaze was cold and it struck fear in me. "It's time you got dusted once and for all."

"I'll take you anytime you want," J.T. bragged. He looked around at his friends. "After football season, though. If you can hold off."

Of course, they all laughed.

"You have messed with the wrong person,

jerk-off," Jason said, his voice still low and men-acing.

J.T. jumped to his feet, knocking his chair backward. "What did you call me?"

Jason didn't move, didn't back up. His mouth was set in a firm line, but his hands hung loosely at his sides. "So you're both dumb *and* deaf, are you?"

I held my breath because I knew J.T. was go-ing to hit Jason, but just then Coach came run-ning over. "What's going on here?"

"Nothing," J.T. said, shrugging his huge shoulders. "Jason had a little accident and thinks it's my fault. He was clumsy and is trying to blame me for it."

Jason didn't say a word but just kept staring into J.T.'s lying face.

"Save it for the field, J.T.," Coach said. "Now sit down." He turned to Jason. "You all right, son?"

"No damage," Jason said.

"Then you go clean up. I'll get a janitor in to mop up the mess." Coach sounded sympathetic, but it made me mad to think he wouldn't do any-thing to J.T. because of the upcoming game. He wouldn't dream of benching his star player.

Jason turned, stepped over the tray and headed out of the cafeteria. I watched with new respect for Jason Polwalski. In all my years, I'd never seen anyone stand up to J. T. Rucker. Jason's bravery made me like him all the more. Really, really like him.

I told Becky all about it when we walked home, except for the part about how much I liked Jason. She said, "Jason's either very brave or very dumb. Taking on J.T. is not for the fainthearted."

"I don't think Jason would have said what he did if he didn't think he could take J.T.," I said.

"J.T.'s got three inches and thirty pounds over Jason, you know."

"So what? The race doesn't always go to the fastest."

"You sound like you've taken a shine to Jason."

My face reddened, but I kept my gaze front-ward. "I'd just love to see somebody give J.T. what he's been needing all his life—a good whipping."

"Sorry, friend," Becky Sue said. "Jason may be brave, but I really don't think he's the one to do it."

I didn't dare say anything or Becky would suspect me of other motives.

Later that afternoon I was working in the yard when someone called my name. I looked up and saw Jason standing on my back porch. I dropped my armful of bush clippings.

"I brought over a casserole from Carole," he

called. "I rang the front bell, but nobody answered. Your front door was unlocked, so I brought it inside. Carole said you were expecting it."

He was walking toward me as he explained.

"Nobody locks their doors in Conners," I told him. I was grubby with yard dirt and sweat. My hair hung in my eyes, and I was certain that I smelled like a wet dog.

He looked around. "Whoa. This place is beautiful. Is it yours?"

"My family's," I said. "Mama can't keep it up now, so I do it for her."

"Can I look around?"

"Sure." I rubbed my dirty hands on my jeans. "Don't they have gardens in Chicago?"

"Not in my neighborhood. Just concrete and asphalt."

His description of home surprised me. I couldn't imagine growing up without grass and trees all around. "Want some iced tea?" I asked, thinking of a way to go inside and make myself presentable and to keep him around a bit longer.

"Everyone drinks iced tea around here. Is it the beverage of the South?"

"That would be RC Cola."

He grinned. "All right. I'll drink some iced tea."

I hurried into the house, where I threw cold

water on my face and brushed my hair. In the mirror, I looked at a skinny, flat-chested girl with blond hair, fine as cornsilk, and a face as plain as brown wrapping paper. Disgusted because I wasn't pretty like Adel, I rushed back to the kitchen and dragged out the iced tea pitcher from the refrigerator. Mama kept sweet tea ready to pour year-round. "It's hospitable," she told us. So even with her away, Adel and I kept up her tradition.

I carried two glasses outside and discovered Jason sitting on the bench overlooking the pond. Cooler weather had caused the vines to die back, but the autumn clematis was in bloom along the fence and looked beautiful with its tiny star-shaped white flowers. I handed him a glass and sat at the farthest end of the bench, my nerve endings tingling.

"That's pretty. What is it?" He was pointing to the flowering vine.

"*Clematis vitalba.* That's its Latin name. It only flowers in the fall."

"I'll bet you know the names of every single plant in this yard, don't you?"

"Mostly," I said. "I love Mama's gardens."

"I don't blame you. They're really pretty." He sipped his tea and continued to look around. "I asked Carole to let me bring over the casserole," he said.

"You did?"

"I wanted to thank you for trying to warn me in the cafeteria today."

"I'm sorry the warning wasn't in time." I traced my finger around the rim of my glass. "You really aren't afraid of J.T., are you?"

Jason shrugged. "I've taken down tougher guys."

"Really? How?"

His eyes held mine. "I fight dirty," he said simply. "But I win."

I didn't know what to say. I'd never heard anybody be quite so frank.

"You don't seem to be afraid of him either," Jason said.

I thought before answering. "I wouldn't rile him on purpose, but most of the time, he makes me more angry than scared. I never did take to people who pick on others just because they're bigger or meaner. And someday, someone's going to come along who's bigger and meaner than J.T. Then he'll get a taste of what he's put everybody else through."

"You're right," Jason said, standing and handing me back the empty iced tea glass. "There's always someone who can take you down."

I didn't want him to leave, but I couldn't figure a way to ask him to stay either. "Thanks for bringing our supper over."

"Like I said, I asked to bring it." He looked around the yard one more time. "And I'm glad I did, or I'd never have seen this place."

I followed him around to the front of the house, where his motorcycle was parked in the driveway. The tea glasses were cold in my hands and the air had turned cooler too. Jason threw his leg over his cycle and brought the engine to life.

"You can come visit anytime," I blurted out.

He measured me with his cool green eyes, waved and pulled away.

Feeling hot and cold all over, I watched him ride off. I brought the glass he had held to my cheek, rested it against my warm skin and shivered.

Three days before Thanksgiving, Mama called. "I have wonderful news," she said. "My doctor is allowing me to come home. Oh, Graham, girls . . . I can come home!"

# Ten

I made a banner that said Welcome Home and Adel and I hung it across the front veranda so that it would be the first thing Mama saw when she and Papa drove up. Becky Sue helped me blow up about a hundred balloons and we hung them all over the house, along with crepe paper streamers. Adel baked a cake—Mama's favorite, lemon chiffon—and polished up the silver coffee service in the dining room in honor of her home-coming.

When they arrived, I bolted out of the house and practically threw myself into Mama's arms. Papa said, "Slow down, missy. You're going to knock your mother over."

She smiled. A bandana covered her head and her clothes hung loosely on her body. "Oh, girls, this is so lovely," she said. "Thank you." She caressed the house and front yard with her gaze. "What a sight for sore eyes. I've missed my family and my home so much."

Her tears caused a lump to rise in my throat. "Come on in, Mama," I said hastily. "We cleaned and cooked and decorated all morning."

Papa helped her up the front porch steps, for she seemed weakened, as if all her vitality had been drained. I grabbed her suitcase out of the car. In the front hallway, she stopped, stood and wept. "I don't ever want to leave this house again until the undertaker comes for me."

No one spoke. The image of the black wreath from Grandmother's funeral appeared in my mind.

Mama sighed and shook her head. "Oh now, where's your sense of humor? I already look half dead and all of you know it. This is a brand-new day and we have company coming for the holiday. What are you girls cooking up for Barry?"

The bank closed midafternoon on Wednesday, and Adel had taken off Friday. Although we had plenty of offers from friends to fix our holiday dinner, Adel and I decided we could do it ourselves. We went to the grocery store together and, armed with lists of ingredients for Mama's recipes, bought bagfuls of groceries.

Wednesday evening, Papa set up one of the

comfortable overstuffed chairs from the living room in the kitchen and Mama sat, curled up with a quilt, and supervised our preparations for the big feast. "Think you've got enough?" Papa asked mildly. He stood beside Mama's chair and surveyed the pots bubbling on the stove and the counters filled with cooling pies and gelatin salads and chopped vegetables ready for cooking.

"I don't want to wait until the last minute," Adel said. "Besides, it's not only Thanksgiving, it's a celebration too. Barry's never eaten my cooking, you know."

I was mincing celery for turkey stuffing. "That might not be a bad thing."

Adel turned on me. "I don't need any smart remarks from you, Darcy Rebecca. Is your room ready for him?"

"Squeaky clean. I changed the sheets, swept the floor, hung up all my clothes."

"And your bathroom?"

"You can eat off the floor."

"What time do you expect Barry?" Mama asked.

"Around ten o'clock. I thought we'd eat around one."

We usually ate our big Thanksgiving feast in the early afternoon, so Adel was sticking to tradition. "Did you get fresh cranberries?" Mama asked.

"And fresh oranges," Adel said. "Darcy's going to grind them together just like you always do."

I pulled the food grinder from the cabinet to reinforce Adel's claim. "We're doing everything just like you always do," I said.

"Goodness . . . you don't even need me."

I knew Mama was trying to encourage our efforts, but none of us had words to tell her just how much we needed her. "I need you," Papa said.

I saw Mama slip her hand into his and him hold on to hers like a man holding a rope so that he wouldn't drown.

Later that night, as I was throwing a quilt over the cot in Adel's room, I said, "I'm glad Mama's home. I've missed her."

"Me too," Adel said.

I yawned and stretched out under the quilt. "Everything is perfect. Mama's home and you haven't burned anything edible."

She threw her hairbrush at me.

Adel set her alarm, rose at six and went down to stuff the turkey and get it in the oven. I pulled the covers over my head. By nine, we were all up helping in the kitchen, even Papa. I set the table with our best family silver and Wedgwood china on Great-Grandmother's finest Irish linen tablecloth. I made a centerpiece of mums from the garden in a silver bowl and set matching silver candelabras with tall white tapers upon the table. I hand polished the mahogany sideboard and chair backs until they gleamed. I was admiring my handiwork when Barry's rental car pulled up in our driveway.

Adel rushed outside to greet him, brought him into the living room and introduced him to Mama. "I've been looking forward to meeting you, Mrs. Quinlin," he said.

"Call me Joy," Mama said, blessing him with her smile.

Barry was dressed in civilian clothing—civvies, he called them—and he looked more handsome than ever. I couldn't wait to show him off to Becky Sue. Eventually I took him upstairs to my room so that he could stash his army duffel bag. "Thanks for giving up your room," he told me, looking around at my spiffed-up quarters. "I would have slept on the floor."

"I'd have slept on the floor first. Hospitality matters. It's the Southern way."

He walked over to my rather large poster project. It was thumbtacked to the longest wall, and it stretched the whole length of it. He examined it closely. "What's this?"

"Special project for my government class," I said. "I've been working on it for weeks, even though it isn't due until May."

"I thought most kids your age put up posters of their favorite rock band." He grinned. "So tell me about it."

I shrugged self-consciously. "I still have to do the written part of the report, but this is a time line of America's involvement in Vietnam. See here?" I pointed to the first date and my neatly written historical notes. "This is 1955, when our country started messing around in the politics after the French were forced out. Here's 1961, when President Kennedy tried to negotiate a settlement between the Communist party holding the north part of Vietnam and the non-Communists in the South. Here's 1963, when things started to escalate after the President was assassinated." I stopped and turned to Barry. "Did you know that Buddhist monks set themselves on fire to protest religious persecution? Can you imagine?"

Barry shook his head. "No, I can't." He ran his finger along the line, reading as he went. " 'August 1964, the Gulf of Tonkin Resolution, U.S.S. *Maddox* battleship attacked and more troops sent. . . . 1965, Operation Rolling Thunder, sustained bombing missions begun by U.S. . . . 1966, North Vietnamese Army crosses Demilitarized Zone and is driven back in heavy fighting. . . .' "

I drew his attention to a second time line I'd drawn in bright red, running beneath the first.

"This is what was happening in this country during the military buildup in Vietnam," I said. "See? In 1965, protesters started marching on college campuses. By 1968, at the Democratic National Convention, there was a free-for-all, with protesters burning flags and draft cards and fighting in the streets of Chicago with police."

Barry ran his hand along both lines but began reading again from the one about the war. " 'Nineteen sixty-seven, the Tet Offensive buildup begins; 1968, the Battle for Khe Sanh.' " He stopped. "Khe Sanh . . . that's the firefight that my brother was in."

"Really?"

"It scarred him for life," Barry said. He looked grim and suddenly I wondered about the wisdom of showing off my project to him. Adel was going to kill me if I ruined Thanksgiving.

"Well, soldiers also started coming back home in sixty-eight," I said, trying to put a positive spin on my chart and pointing to my notations.

"But the war spilled over into Cambodia and Laos," he said, following a branch of the time line shooting off one side dated 1970 and 1971. I had made factual addendums to the chart about Vietnam's neighboring countries and the encroachment of the war over their borders.

"Yes, but by 1972, all but a third of U.S. troops were pulled out," I said, talking fast to finish up because I could see that he was determined to follow the chart to its conclusion. "In January 1973, we signed the Paris Peace Agreement. And in March 1973, our combat soldiers left and today only military advisors and troops protecting U.S. installations remain."

"And that's where your time line stops," Barry said.

"Because the war is up to the Vietnamese to finish," I said. "I'm not sure how to end my project. Doesn't seem right not to give it an ending."

"Maybe you should write the North and South Vietnamese governments and ask them to get it over with so you can turn this in."

I smiled. "Maybe so."

He ran his fingers over boxes I'd drawn at the bottom of the chart. "What do you plan to put here?"

"Casualties," I admitted. "Another reason to get the war over with. So that people can stop dying."

With Barry scrutinizing my project, it took on a face and gained substance for me. Real people had died in Vietnam—brothers, fathers, sons, husbands—living, breathing men. Until that moment, my chart had been an abstract exercise to win a better grade. But seeing it through Barry's eyes had turned it into a chronicle not only of history, but of people's lives.

Barry stepped away from the wall, shoved his hands in his pockets. "You've done a good job, Darcy. If I were your teacher, I'd give you an A-plus."

"Thank you," I said, feeling a heaviness in my heart.

"There you are!" Adel swept into the room. "Did Darcy kidnap you?"

Barry put his arm around her. "I was just looking over one of her school projects. She's a bright girl."

Adel eyed my chart suspiciously, then turned back to Barry. "I wondered if you'd like to come down and join my parents while Darcy and I finish up the meal."

I understood the message she was sending about needing my help.

"Sounds good," Barry said.

They left hand in hand. I waited a few minutes before following them downstairs. Afternoon sunlight filtered through the curtains in the dining room and the aroma of turkey filled our house, yet all I could think of were the soldiers who would never have Thanksgiving dinner again because they were no more.

# Eleven

By the time we demolished Thanksgiving dinner, I was feeling more cheerful. I really *was* thankful that our family was together. Barry seemed at ease at our table. Papa said, "Nice to have another male voice around. Sometimes I can't get a word in edgewise, with all these women talking." Papa always liked to tease us about our chatter, but I knew he was grateful to hear it again after Mama's long absence.

I carried the plates and dishes to the kitchen, where Barry insisted on rolling up his sleeves and helping Adel load the dishwasher and scrub the pots and pans. "But you're a guest," Adel said. "Darcy can help me."

"I'm pretty good at this," Barry said. "The army's taught me well. Come on. You and me, babe."

I happily left them to their work and returned to the living room, where Papa had set up the card table and Mama was busy spreading out a new one-thousand-piece puzzle. That was what we did on holidays and rainy days—we worked jigsaw puzzles and played board games. Everyone would pitch in on the puzzle and after a time drift off and do something else, then return to check the progress and slip a few more pieces into place. The card table was often up for days until the puzzle was completed.

We had pieced together about half of the border when the doorbell rang. I went to find Becky Sue on the veranda. "Where is he?" were the first words out of her mouth.

"And happy Thanksgiving to you too," I said, letting her into the house. "In the kitchen," I added. "Dishes are done, but they haven't come out yet."

She followed me into the kitchen, where Barry and Adel were sitting and peering into each other's eyes like lovesick puppies. After introductions, Becky and I went up to Adel's room, where she hooked her arm around the bedpost and said, "What a hunk! Your sister is so lucky."

"He's nice too. Talks to me like I'm a real person with opinions that count. Her boyfriends from high school treated me like a pest that needed shooing."

"So what's he do in the army?"

"Something with radios and satellites. He can't talk about it much."

"Won't the army send him away?"

"Sure."

"It's going to break Adel's heart to lose *that* one."

"What makes you think she'll lose him? Just because he leaves doesn't mean they won't write and call each other."

"Depends on where they send him," Becky said. "What if he goes off to some country where there's lots of free love?"

"You see too many movies," I said, but her questions nibbled at me the rest of the day.

Once we all drifted up to bed, I waited until Adel came out of her bathroom and asked her the same thing Becky had asked me. "What will you and Barry do when the army sends him far away?"

Adel turned down her bed. "We'll write."

"Aren't you afraid he'll meet someone else?"

"If some other girl can take him away from me, then we didn't have much going on between us, now, did we?"

Her confidence was inspiring. I wondered if I'd ever feel that secure about another person's feelings. "Well, what about him being in the army? Do you worry about him getting hurt?"

"The army will take care of him. And they're

not sending troops to Vietnam anymore, so he won't be in harm's way." She scooted under the covers. "I think it would be fun to travel all over the world. I'd love to see Paris and Rome."

"Is that why you like him? So that he can send you postcards from around the world?"

"Don't be silly. I like him because of who he is. He's the most wonderful man in the world."

"Why do you suppose he joined the army? I mean, after what happened to his brother and all."

"Duty," she said simply. "All the men in his family have served in the military. Barry grew up wanting to serve his country. That's part of who he is." Adel flipped off the bedside lamp.

I told her good night and turned over, only to gaze out the window and see a brilliant pale white moon gleaming down. The image of Jason's face floated across my mind's eye. I wondered what his holiday had been like, if he'd been happy, if he'd missed his family in Chicago. And I wondered if he had thought of me even once.

"Honey, you've done such a fine job. All the dead leaves raked up and the pansies planted. Thank you." Mama and I were navigating the backyard and looking over my handiwork. Adel and Barry had driven off to scout the town right after breakfast, and I had told Becky I'd come over in the afternoon.

"The flowers do look pretty, don't they?" I said, feeling satisfied with myself for making Mama happy. The pansies looked cheerful in the freshly mulched beds, their colorful faces turned up to catch the sun. Pansies bloomed all winter this far south because we rarely got snow, or even lingering frosts. The flowers thrived until the wilting heat came in late spring and made them fade. Mama always planted them for color.

I said, "I thought about pruning back the crepe myrtle, but I remembered that you usually do that in February."

"That's right. You're such a good gardener, Darcy."

Her praise made my heart swell. "I wasn't sure about the roses, Mama."

"Yes, they can be a problem, yet they're so lovely you can forgive them and their sulky ways."

I giggled. "You talk as if they're human."

"They think they are, and I'd never tell them otherwise." Her arm was looped through mine and we were wearing heavy sweaters, but her arm felt feather light. She wore a kind of turban around her head, and dangling gold earrings that caught the sun. "I should get the yardman to sow some winter rye," she said. "For the green color."

The grass, a variety that died back in cold weather, was turning brown. Our yardman cut, edged and fertilized the grass, while Mama kept the gardens. "Maybe we can go up to the nursery and buy a few more flats of pansies," she said. "It's not too late to get more planted, and I think I'd like more color in the beds below the back porch."

"We can go tomorrow," I said. "I'll get them in the ground next week."

"Don't neglect your schoolwork."

"I'm caught up," I said. "Even ahead in some classes."

Mama stopped walking. "Let me catch my breath. Goodness. . . . I've been lying in bed much too long. I'm out of shape."

Alarmed, I said, "Maybe we should go inside."

"All I do inside is answer the phone and tell well-meaning friends that I'm doing all right."

"Then let's sit in the swing," I offered. "You really are all right, aren't you, Mama?"

She patted my hand. "I have a ways to go before I get my strength back, but yes, I'm okay."

I felt relieved. Soon things would be back to normal and our lives would pick up from where we'd put them on hold when Mama had been diagnosed with breast cancer.

Mama tipped back her head, took deep

breaths. "Is there anything in God's world more beautiful than flowers and trees?"

I knew she wasn't asking me a real question, just thinking out loud.

"One more thing, Darcy. I'm turning over my garden club presidency to Mrs. Teasdale."

"But why? You love the club."

"And I still do. But Wicki Teasdale will take it over. I want to concentrate on my family and on feeling good again. I don't think I can tackle the garden show in April."

"But you always do the show." I was dismayed by Mama's withdrawal.

"It takes great effort to get it together. I've already missed months of work. Wicki will do just fine. She'll be by this week to pick up all my records and files. It's best this way, honey."

I knew that relinquishing her presidency wasn't an easy thing for my mother to do. She'd been at the helm of that club ever since I could remember. Even when Grandmother was sick, she'd participated. "I'll help you, Mama. You don't have to quit," I said.

"I won't hear of it," she said quietly. "It's time for me to step down, make room for others. It's okay, Darcy. It's what I want."

I wanted to believe her, but all I could think was that this was one more thing breast cancer had stolen from my mother. "But sometime soon, teach me how to deal with the roses and their sulky ways. All right?"

Her smile seemed to come from far away. "Lesson number one, honey. Roses take time . . . a whole lot of time."

Adel and Barry didn't get home until supper-time and were up and eating breakfast when I came down at nine on Saturday. They kept giving each other adoring puppy-dog stares, and Adel was so sugary sweet that I was glad diabetes wasn't catching like the flu. They eventually left for a drive, and I spent the afternoon at Becky's.

Walking home that evening, I thought about Mama, and school, and Jason, and how I was going to continue hiding my feelings for him from Becky Sue because I didn't want to be teased. And tease me she would. I deserved it too, for hadn't I poked fun at her for years over her numerous crushes?

I turned the corner and saw Barry's rental car in the driveway, which meant Adel was home. I jogged up the porch steps and banged open the front door—sounding like a herd of elephants, I was certain. *Who wants a girlfriend who clumps?* I purposely slowed my entrance into the kitchen, where I saw Mama and Papa sitting at the table with Barry and Adel. I asked, "What's happening?" for I could tell by their expressions that *something* was happening.

"You're just in time," Adel cried, her smile as bright as sunshine. She held out her left hand, where a small diamond ring sparkled in the light. "Barry's asked me to marry him, and I've said yes, yes, yes!"

# Twelve

## December

"**Married!** Really? When?" The words tumbled out of my mouth.

"Slow down, girl," Papa said. "That's just what we were discussing."

I hugged Adel, then Barry. "This is so far out. I—I can't believe it."

"I think she's glad about it," Adel said to Barry.

He grinned and threw his free arm around my shoulders. His other arm was around Adel, of course. "Not as glad as I am," he said. "I've been on pins and needles for weeks, knowing I was going to propose." He looked at our parents. "Thank you for giving us your blessing."

Mama took Papa's hand. Tears had filled her eyes. "We're very happy for you both," she said.

"The ring belonged to Barry's grandmother," Adel said, flashing it again.

"I asked my mother to send it weeks ago," Barry explained. "She always told me it would be mine to give to the girl of my dreams."

Barry's open adoration caused a lump in my throat.

"Have you set a date?" Papa asked, getting back to the practical side of the event.

Adel and Barry exchanged quick glances. Adel scooted closer to Mama. "Don't panic, but we want to get married at Christmas."

Mama blanched. "Christmas? *This* Christmas?"

"The Lockheed project will be finished and I'll be getting my orders right after the first of the year," Barry said. "I love Adel very much, and I want her to be my wife before I leave. If I get sent to a base in Europe, she'll be able to come with me."

"But your mother's health—" Papa began.

"Not now, Graham," Mama interrupted.

"I'll plan everything," Adel said in an impassioned voice. "Mama won't have to worry about it. I don't want a big fancy wedding. Just something small with family and maybe a few friends. How hard can it be? I'll even buy my own dress— again, nothing elaborate. We'll have the reception in the church fellowship hall—cake and punch, some nuts and those little butter mints will be fine. I don't want to go to a country club in Atlanta like Mary Teasdale did. I just want to become Barry's wife in the shortest amount of time, with the least amount of fuss."

I almost asked why she and Barry hadn't eloped if they didn't want to create a fuss, but didn't because I'd only sound contentious and I was happy for Adel. I really was.

Mama held up her hand. "I don't want my firstborn daughter to skimp on her wedding."

"But I don't *want* a big fancy wedding," Adel insisted.

"My parents will be the only ones who'll come from New York," Barry said. "And I'll invite a few of my army buddies and my commander. That's about it for me."

"What about your brother?" Mama asked.

"Kyle's in a VA hospital, and—" He paused. "Well, we don't expect him to be out anytime soon."

The back of my neck felt prickly because I knew about his brother and Vietnam and how his war experience had changed his life.

"See, Mama," Adel said. "A small wedding won't be any trouble at all."

"I want you to have what you want, honey," Mama said. "We'll talk it out later. For now, you two just go be happy."

When they'd left the kitchen, Papa said, "Are you really up to this? I worry about you. . . ."

Mama patted his hand. "Goodness, I'm not fine china and I won't break." She reached up, removed the wall calendar and flipped the page. "Sunday is December first. That gives us three and a half weeks until Christmas. Why, the Good Lord created the entire universe in seven days. Surely we can put on a small wedding in twenty-five."

Saturday night, after Barry had returned to the base, I told Adel again how happy I was for her. She'd been talking to Mama about the wedding and now stood in the doorway of my reclaimed bedroom.

I asked, "Who'll be in your wedding?" I'd only attended one wedding in my lifetime, and that had been for the daughter of one of Mama's friends when I was ten. It had been an enormous affair with seven bridesmaids, seven groomsmen, a flower girl and a ring bearer—at the time, I thought they all would *never* get down the aisle.

"I've already asked Sandy to be my maid of honor, and Barry's friend Mason will be Barry's best man." Adel turned to me. "And you'll be my bridesmaid. That's about it for the wedding party."

I choked on the gum still in my mouth. "Me? A bridesmaid?"

"Don't look so shocked. You're my sister. Of course you'll be my bridesmaid."

I understood then. It was expected of her to ask me. Why, our parents would raise the roof if she didn't ask me. "I think I'd rather sit on the sidelines," I said.

"Nonsense." Adel came over and took my chin in her hand and turned my face in several directions, all the while looking me over. "You'll have to wear some makeup," she said.

"But I don't like—"

"Hush, and listen to me. Some blush and a swipe of eye shadow, a little lipstick, and with your hair up you'll look twice your age. It's time you fixed yourself up a little, Darcy. You're a pretty girl and you need to take advantage of it."

Her no-nonsense voice told me it would be useless to argue. But my feelings were hurt. I could be in her wedding—I *had* to be in her wedding— but I'd have to look the way Adel wanted me to look. I pulled away from her hand. "Will you promise me one thing, Adel? Will you please not put me in head-to-toe pink ruffles?"

She laughed gaily. "Silly girl. Pink is no color for a Christmas wedding."

She turned out the light and left me to

wonder in the dark if she was joking or serious. Sometimes with Adel, I couldn't figure it out.

The minute church let out the next morning, I found Becky Sue and told her the news.

"Why didn't you call and tell me last night? How could you have kept this from me until now?"

"Adel was on the phone all evening. Besides, I wanted to see your face when I told you."

"And so you have. Tell me everything."

"Don't know much yet. It's still in the planning stages."

"Can I come?"

I shrugged. "It's supposed to be real small."

"But I have to come! I want to come!"

"I'll do what I can." I thought it best to mollify her. We didn't need her pitching a hissy fit in the church hall. "I'm going to be a bridesmaid," I added.

"How romantic," she crooned. "When will you pick out your dress?"

"We're going to Atlanta next weekend to shop."

We went outdoors, where people were standing and talking in spite of the chilly December wind. The sky hung gray over us and clouds resembled dark smudges like marks left by a dirty eraser. Shivering, I told Becky goodbye and started for the parking lot, where I saw that Papa and Mama were already sitting in the car, warming it up.

"Heard Adel is getting married," a voice said from behind me. "And in a big hurry too. Makes people wonder why she's marrying so quickly."

J.T. was wearing a smirk when I turned to face him. "You won't be invited to the wedding," I said, my voice dripping with ice.

"Who cares. Is she knocked up?"

I could have clawed his eyes out. "She's in love, J.T.," I said through clenched teeth. "Nothing you'd know about though, because you have a small mind and a big dirty mouth." I felt brave because I knew my parents were watching us.

"You're fun to poke at," he said with a laugh. "My guess is that that soldier boy has already taken a poke at Adel."

My face flushed as I caught the double meaning of the word "poke." I squared my chin. "You are crude and rude, J. T. Rucker. Nothing but white trash."

I hurried to the car with him laughing meanly in my wake. I jerked open the door and slammed it hard behind me.

"What's wrong?" Papa asked.

"J. T. Rucker makes me crazy mad. He's hateful and nasty. He asked me if Adel was getting married because she had to—you know—*had* to."

I let the implication sink in because I was suddenly embarrassed to say the word "pregnant" to my parents.

"People are going to think what they want to think," Papa said mildly.

"Doesn't it bother you?" I was shocked that neither he nor Mama took offense.

"Yes, but because I don't want anyone thinking ill of my daughter. Fact is, the bigger stink you raise denying something, the more entrenched people become in their own viewpoint about it. As to the issue of Adel's timing of her wedding, time will tell the gossips that they were wrong, so we don't have to." Papa's voice was firm.

"J.T.'s just being spiteful because Adel would never give him the time of day," I grumbled.

Mama glanced in the rearview mirror. "Just put it out of your mind, Darcy. We have enough other things to think about."

I hunkered down in the seat. It was good that the two of them didn't have to confront gossip and innuendo, but at school I'd be up against it every day. Everybody would be asking the same question once J.T. got the rumor mill going. And there was no doubt in my mind that he would get it going. No doubt at all.

"Most people are real happy for Adel," Becky Sue assured me Monday afternoon as we walked home from school. She had kept her ear tuned for hall gossip all day about my sister's engagement and fast-approaching wedding date. I had been certain it was the sole topic of conversation that day, because whenever I entered a room or went into a bathroom, talk stopped and all eyes turned to me. Everybody looked guilty of spreading rumors.

"Donna and her friends aren't happy," I said. "They just look smirky," I added with distaste.

"What do you expect? J.T. snaps his fingers and Donna jumps," Becky said. "Just remember, Conners is small and Adel is our local celebrity. People are interested in her business. Her wedding is news."

"Her wedding, yes, but they have no right to say the other part."

"What's so terrible about having a baby less than nine months after the wedding? This is the seventies!"

I gave her a sidelong glance. "You don't think that, do you? About Adel needing to get married quick because she might be pregnant?"

"No," Becky Sue said, but I thought I saw her gaze shift. "People just talk," she added. "Ignore them."

Easy for her to say. It wasn't her sister.

# Thirteen

⤷⤛ ⤛⤜

"Thank you for coming, Carole. I really need to talk," I heard my mama say as she brought Carole onto the back porch.

They couldn't see me because I was below them in the flower bed that sloped downward from under the porch. I was planting two flats of pansies like Mama had wanted me to do. It was late afternoon at the end of the first week in December. The day had turned out pleasant, sunny and bright, more like early fall, perfect for putting in the last of the flowers.

Carole said, "I'm glad you called. You're so much on my mind."

I heard the sound of chairs being pulled out from the table on the porch. Guiltily, I decided against standing up and announcing myself. I kept scooping up dirt with my small spade and tucking the colorful pansies into the ground, telling myself that I wouldn't listen in.

"I need help with Adel's wedding," I heard Mama say. "We've got less than three weeks. There are so many details—flowers, music, written announcements, the cake. . . ." Mama took a breath. "I know Adel thinks she's going to handle it, but she works all day. She has no idea how much work there is in organizing a wedding. Even a small one."

"Don't you worry about a thing. All you have to do is make lists. I'll do the rest. Jim will get together with Adel, and Barry, if possible, and work out details for the ceremony. I'll get the Women's Circle to plan and set up the fellowship hall for the reception. Leave everything to me."

I could picture Carole comforting Mama.

"I'm just so tired," Mama said after a pause. "I want to feel good again. I can't even recall the last day I felt good. I want to be there for Adel at her wedding."

My heart felt as if it were being squeezed. Mama never complained.

"What have the doctors told you?"

My spade stopped in midair. I sat back on my heels, knowing that eavesdropping was wrong, but I couldn't stop myself.

"They've told me that what I'm feeling is normal for a person with my condition. Normal,"

Mama repeated. "I hope I never experience ab-
normal."

"We'll get them to refine their vocabulary, all
right?" I heard sympathy in Carole's voice.

"Just get me through this wedding, Carole.
That's all I ask."

"Of course."

After a minute, Mama said, "I feel as if I've
been neglectful of my friends. I'm sorry."

"Please don't apologize. It's not necessary."

"How's your brother doing? I know how con-
cerned you were about him coming."

My ears pricked up at the mention of Jason.

Carole said, "He hasn't exactly fit in. Jim and
I are disappointed. We really thought that bring-
ing him here would make a difference in his life.
But so far it hasn't."

"Yet he's not hanging with a youth gang like
he was in Chicago," Mama said. "You've got to
believe that's better."

"In most ways, it is. Mother wrote to say that
one of his old gang buddies was in jail and another
in the hospital after a knife fight. So, yes, Jason's
better off because his life's not in constant danger,
but he's a loner here. He hasn't made a single
friend."

"That takes time. Especially in a town the size
of Conners. It's a failing, I admit."

"But Conners is small and safe. A good place

to raise a family. And you made me feel welcome when I was a stranger. I'm grateful for that."

They were quiet, giving me a chance to mull over what I was hearing. Nothing I didn't know about Jason, but still, having it confirmed depressed me.

"Any ideas for my kid brother?" I heard Carole ask.

"Does he like school?" Mama wanted to know.

"According to his teachers, he's smart enough, but unmotivated. I didn't have to move him to Conners to know that much."

"Any interest in college?"

"Not that he's expressed, and with this being his final year, I don't think college is in his future. He did like your gardens, though. I sent him over with a casserole one afternoon and Darcy gave him the grand tour."

"Bring him back in the spring when it really looks like something."

"How will you keep it up?" Carole asked.

I assumed they were speaking of the yard.

"Darcy does a good job, but come spring, I'll have to have help."

Mama's statement surprised me. Didn't she think the two of us could do it together?

"It's hard letting go of the things you love," Mama said.

"Very hard," Carole said in agreement.

Silence. My legs were cramping and my feet had gone to sleep from sitting on them, but I didn't dare move.

Finally Carole's voice said, "Come on inside with me, Joy. Your hands are cold as ice. I'll fix you a cup of hot tea."

"I should fix you tea," Mama said.

"Well, if I'm going to help with that wedding, then you'd better get used to me being your arms and legs for a time."

I heard their chairs scraping back.

When I was certain they had gone into the kitchen, I straightened out my legs and felt the prickly sensation in my feet as blood returned to them. I wasn't sure what-all I had heard. Problem was, there was no one I could discuss it with either. Becky Sue would grill me for every detail and I didn't want to share every detail. Adel would bite my head off for snooping. Papa would probably ground me for eavesdropping on a private conversation. I'd have to keep it all to myself and try to sort it out on my own.

On Saturday we went to Atlanta to shop for dresses. Sandy had to work and couldn't come with us. Adel drove and I read directions to the shops she wanted to visit. Mama rested in the backseat. We found nothing to Adel's liking in the first store. We ate lunch in a fancy tearoom, and I saw Mama take several pills.

The next store was carpeted all in white and looked as sugary as a wedding cake. The saleswoman sat us down and took notes about the wedding from Adel. "A nice white suit will be fine," my sister told the saleswoman when it came time to try on dresses, but the woman kept hauling in beaded gowns with puffy sleeves and long trains.

"Why buy a suit when you'll look so pretty in a real dress?" the lady said.

I could tell by the look in Adel's eyes that she was getting seduced, and that her small, no-fuss wedding was growing more elaborate in her mind.

"What do you think, Mama?" Adel asked. She was still wearing the latest try-on, a soft white satin gown that draped to the floor, with seed pearls, ruching on the bodice, and a train trimmed in white rabbit fur.

Mama was in a nice comfortable chair and she seemed more alert than on the drive over. "I want you to have anything you want, Adel. You'll remember your wedding day forever, and it should be the day of your dreams."

"Barry will be in his dress uniform," Adel mused, turning in front of the mirror. "Maybe a suit isn't formal enough."

I was sitting on the floor and thumbing through a bridal magazine. Adel could wear a sack and look lovely.

"What do you think, Darcy?" Adel asked.

I nodded agreeably. "Looks good."

"Why don't you and Darcy try on dresses?" Adel said to Mama. "Maybe if I see the two of you dressed up, it'll help me decide what I want."

"That's not the way it's done," the saleswoman started. "The bride is the focus."

But Adel was already pawing through the racks. She held up a floor-length midnight-blue velvet sheath with long sleeves and a deep V neckline. "Try this on, Darcy," she said, shoving it toward me.

The saleslady perked up. "Oh, that's a wonderful selection."

I wasn't so sure. I preferred jeans and loose tops. My dresses had full skirts because I didn't like the way my bony hips stuck out. But I had promised myself that I would be agreeable all day, so I shut myself in a dressing room and slipped into the dress. When I stepped out of the dressing room, Mama and Adel stared at me without saying a word. "What's wrong?" I asked, glancing down to see if I'd put it on backward.

"Oh my goodness," Mama said.

I faced the three-sided mirror. I didn't

recognize myself. The girl looking back was a vision in blue velvet, slim and soft-looking, like a
fine oil painting in a museum. The dress hugged
my body, except for the top. The saleswoman
rushed forward and expertly pinned it around the
upper bodice. My "bosom" didn't fill it out, she
noted, but it could be easily fixed.

Adel walked around me. "It's not pink ruffles,"
she said. "Disappointed?"

My face reddened.

"Do you like it, Darcy?" she asked.

I lifted my fine blond hair off my shoulders
and held it up, the way I knew she wanted me to
wear it, and stared back at the mirror. I was trans-
formed again. I had never owned anything so
beautiful nor felt so grown up as I did in the dress.
"Yes," I told her. "I like it very much."

"Me too," Adel said. "What do you think,
Mama?" We both turned to face her, me in blue
velvet, Adel in wedding white.

Tears welled in our mother's eyes, and her gaze
lingered on both of us, as if she were taking a pho-
tograph and storing it in a memory box. "You are
both beautiful beyond words," she said softly. "My
dear, darling daughters. I love you with all my
heart. And I always will. Please don't ever forget
that."

I saw emotion brimming in Adel's expression
over our mother's soulful words, and a chill crept

through me that I could neither explain nor banish.

Becky Sue had a fit over the dress when it arrived at the house by special delivery a week later. When I put it on and modeled it for her, she clapped. "It's gorgeous! I mean it, Darcy, you look like a movie star."

"High praise from a girl who likes movies as much as you," I kidded. I whirled and smoothed the front of the dress. I loved the sensuous feel of the material on my palm. "Course, it had to be taken in six inches to accommodate my pathetic little boobs," I added. "I have enough fabric left over to make a pair of gloves."

"Now, you stop ragging on yourself," Becky said, wagging her finger at me.

"Mama said I can wear her sapphire-and-diamond pendant and sapphire earrings," I said. "Adel's wearing Mama's pearls."

"I can't believe I have to miss the wedding," Becky said, looking petulant. Adel had agreed to let Becky Sue and her parents attend, but since it was on Christmas day, her family would be in Kentucky visiting relatives. Becky wasn't happy about it. "Make sure your pictures are developed in time for the New Year's Eve party," she reminded me. "I want to see everything."

"Yes . . . the party. Too bad I can't wear this," I

said, still looking at myself in the mirror. Patti Stephans, one of our classmates, was moving in January and her parents had agreed to let her have a huge farewell party at their summer cabin on Lake Jackson. She'd already invited most of the high school, and Becky Sue had made me swear that I would go with her. Russell was definitely going to be there, according to her sources. "Guess I'll lose Cinderella and turn back into plain ol' Darcy," I said with a sigh.

"Nothing wrong with plain ol' Darcy," Becky said.

Once Becky left, I went down the hall to Mama and Papa's bedroom. I wanted to try on the jewelry with the dress, and frankly, I liked the way the dress made me look and feel, so I wasn't in a hurry to take it off and hang it up.

Mama's bedroom door was ajar. Without thinking, I pushed it open and swept inside, saying, "Mama, can I try on the jewelry—" That was as far as I got.

Mama was dressing. Her slacks were on, but her upper body was uncovered. She ducked down and covered herself with her arms, half turning to shield her nakedness.

"I'm so sorry!" I cried. "I—I didn't mean to burst in on you." I had not seen my mother unclothed since I was a small child. I jumped back into the hall.

Mama's voice stopped me. "Darcy, it's all right. Please come in."

My heart pounded and my cheeks burned. Keeping my gaze downward, I reentered the room.

"I think you should see this, Darcy." Her voice was soft and soothing, much as it had been when I was younger and bruised by a mishap.

My mother had turned to face me from across the room. I didn't want to look, but I did. Her nude upper body was illuminated by lamplight, as the sun had gone down. I glanced at her one perfect breast, then stared at the spot where her other breast had been. In its place was a long diagonal scar cutting across the landscape of her body, marring the flesh like jagged glass. Surgeons had cut off this womanly part of her and left a bright red scar that circled clear under her arm. I could barely stand to look at it, yet neither could I tear my gaze away.

I don't know how long I stood staring, but eventually she slipped on a blouse and came over to me. She ran her thumb under my eyes and down my cheeks. "Don't cry, honey," she said.

Until that moment, I hadn't known I was crying. "What have they done to you, Mama?"

"They have tried to save my life," she answered. "It is only a body part, Darcy. It's no different than a person losing an arm. Or an appendix. There is no shame in it. I wear a special bra that fills me out and makes me appear normal to all the world. No one can tell what's missing when I'm dressed."

I felt the fabric of the velvet dress tight across my chest and I shuddered. At that moment, I was glad my breasts were small and inconsequential. At that moment, I wanted them to go away altogether. I wanted to be as flat as a child and free of them.

My mother read my mind. She lifted my chin and peered into my eyes, her gaze steady and strong. "Do not wish away your womanhood, Darcy Rebecca. Someday, when your time comes, you will revel in your femininity. Being a woman is a most wonderful gift from God. Trust me on this."

I nodded, but my chin was trembling. My mother held me and I felt the hollow place on her chest press against me while I wept.

# Fourteen

Barry was granted a weeklong furlough so that he could marry Adel and have a short honeymoon, a flight to New York to visit his family. The wedding, however, took on a life of its own and the guest list grew like dandelions in spring grass. The details were swallowing us whole, so I made a giant chart to keep track of the plans for the weeks before and after the wedding. I hung it in the kitchen for everybody to see.

*Friday: Darcy out of school for Christmas break. Adel's last day of work at the bank.*

*Saturday: Call Carole for instructions. Follow her instructions.*

*Sunday: 11:00 A.M.—Church. Call Carole/decorating party at fellowship hall (no teen group meeting).*

*Monday:* Barry rents car and picks up his parents at the airport.

*Tuesday:* Barry and parents drive to Conners. NOTE: Christmas Eve!!! Dinner for all of us at our house (Carole cooks).

    7:00 P.M.—Church candlelight service.

    9:00 P.M.—Open Christmas presents.

*Wednesday:* CHRISTMAS DAY!!!!! WEDDING DAY!!!!

    8:00–1:00 P.M.—Eat, bathe, fuss with hair, eat, fuss with makeup, just plain fuss with dresses, flowers, all other stuff.

    2:00 P.M.—The Wedding!!!

    3:00–4:30 P.M.—The Reception.

    5:00 P.M.—Return to house, Barry packs car, say goodbye to Adel and Barry and his family.

    7:50 P.M.—The newly reorganized Sorenson clan flies to New York.

    *Quinlin clan crashes!*

*Monday—(December 30):* Adel and Barry back from honeymoon.

    2:00 P.M.—Adel and Barry arrive in Conners to pack Adel's belongings and return to army base (where they will live happily ever after and until Barry gets sent to parts as yet unknown).

*Monday—(January 6, 1975):* School starts.

*Chart subject to change without notice.*

*Signed:* Darcy Quinlin, creative director and resident sister to the bride

We probably couldn't have managed if it hadn't been for Carole and Mama's network of friends. Carole was Mama's right hand, which was absolutely necessary, because the closer Adel got to her big day, the more she ceased to function as a productive part of the team. "Mama!" she'd wail. "A Christmas wedding—what was I thinking? Why didn't you stop me?"

And Mama would look up from whatever she was doing and say, "Wild horses couldn't have stopped you, Adel. Now go help Carole."

By Christmas Eve, things were running pretty smoothly. We did a quick rehearsal in the afternoon, then ate supper with Barry's folks, whom I liked but could hardly understand due to their thick New York accents. We spent a lot of time saying "Pardon me" and "Could you say again?" and "Sorry, didn't catch your meaning." After dinner, we attended church and came home for dessert and coffee, and then Barry drove his folks to the parsonage to stay with Jim and Carole for the night because there were no motels in Conners and only a boardinghouse where passersthrough stayed, which Mama didn't consider "fit." Barry returned to the house because he was staying in my room as he had at Thanksgiving, and, together, we opened Christmas presents.

I had known it would be a small Christmas, what with the wedding and all, so I was totally surprised when Mama and Papa gave me exactly what I had wanted—a new portable stereo record player, the kind with a tape deck in it. I'd used Adel's old player for years and it was wearing out.

My surprise showed because Adel said, "Why, Darcy, were you afraid Santa might pass you by?"

"Actually, I was afraid Santa would take one peek through the window and go away."

The living room was stacked high with gifts. Not only because it was Christmas, but also because people were sending wedding presents. Papa had set up a table for the wedding loot—all un-opened because Adel had been waiting for Barry to arrive—and the table was heaped and over-flowing onto the floor. "It'll take you a month to open all of them," I said, gesturing at the table.

"Opening presents wasn't on the kitchen chart," Barry said with a straight face. "We'll have to do it when we get back from our honeymoon."

"What's your apartment like?" Mama asked.

"It's near the base where plenty of military couples rent," Barry answered. "We'll take a fur-nished place until we know where the army's go-ing to send me. I should get my orders soon."

"In the meantime, we'll leave our new things here," Adel added. "Once we know where we're going, the army will ship it for us."

The room went quiet as the magnitude of what was happening pressed against us. Adel was leaving home and perhaps going very far away. Like seeds in the wind, our family was being scattered.

Papa broke the mood when he bent down and retrieved a slim box from under the tree. "I believe this has your name on it, Mrs. Quinlin."

"For me?" Mama smiled, delighted.

"My one and only," Papa said.

She opened the box and drew out a diamond bracelet that made the rest of us gawk. It sparkled in the light from the tree. "Oh, my," Mama whispered. "It's stunning." She kissed Papa and hugged him. "Graham, you shouldn't have."

"Yes, I should have." He fastened the bracelet around her wrist. "This is what you have to look forward to, Barry. Spending half a year's salary just to see your beloved's face light up."

"Seems worth every penny," Barry said, squeezing Adel's hand.

Later, when it appeared that everything had been opened and we were starting upstairs, Barry handed me one last box. "This is specially for you, Darcy. It's not exactly a Christmas present, but it's something I want you to have."

Mystified, I opened it and pulled out a scrapbook, filled with writing and photographs of soldiers. "Who are they?"

"This is my brother's. I had Mom bring it. It's pictures from his tour of duty in Vietnam."

My breath caught. "Really?"

"I thought you could use it for that government project you're doing. You can look it over later. These photos tell a story you might not have gotten through your other research."

"Won't he miss it?"

"Not now. I'll get it back from you once school's out. Take care of it, okay?"

"With my life," I declared. "Thank you, Barry. Thank you *so much*."

His expression was one of sadness. "Someday, maybe these veterans will be honored the way they should have been when they came home, instead of being spit on. Who knows? Maybe someday we'll even build a memorial to them."

I hugged the book to my chest and hurried up the stairs. From the back of the hallway, I saw a light coming from my parents' bedroom and decided I'd be the first to say merry Christmas, for by now it was past midnight. The door was ajar, but before I could knock, I heard Papa's voice sounding imploring and respectful. I knew at once that he was praying. Usually, he prayed aloud at church meetings, or at the table before meals. Once, when I'd been sick as a child, he'd knelt by my bed and prayed for me, and the very next morning I woke up fever free. Unable to stop myself, I peeked around the doorjamb.

Papa was on his knees beside the bed where

Mama lay. His head was bowed and his hands were clasped around hers. Mama's eyes were closed. Lamplight bathed them both in a shimmer of gold. Papa was saying, "And bless Adel's wedding day, dear Lord. Let her and Barry have a long and fruitful marriage. And one more thing I ask, Heavenly Father . . . in the name of Jesus, let my beloved wife have a happy and pain-free day."

I didn't want to break the spell, so I backed quietly away from the door. I returned to Adel's room down the hall, whispering my papa's prayer with every step, trying to hold back my tears.

Christmas day dawned bright and sunny, but bitter cold. Carole arrived at the house real early, and the first thing she did was make Papa and Barry leave. Something about the groom not seeing the bride before the ceremony, which didn't make much sense to me. They grabbed up their wedding clothes and headed to the parsonage to have breakfast with Barry's folks.

Sandy arrived, and she and Adel commenced to scurrying around like Chicken Little. Carole told Mama to stay in bed awhile longer, but she wouldn't. "I want to help," Mama said. "I feel just fine." So Carole sat her down to make floral arrangements for the reception tables from roses and white poinsettias sent over by the florist.

Around noon, Adel sat me down and started

applying makeup while Sandy did my hair. Every few minutes, Adel would say, "Stop squirming, Darcy, or you'll look like a clown. I can't hit a moving target."

At some point we were all ready. Papa came home with Simon Ledbetter, the photographer, who took all kinds of photographs of us. He posed us on the stairs, Adel at the foot, holding her bouquet, with her long train cascading onto the floor, then me one step up, and Mama another step higher. Mama was dressed in pale blue wool, a matching turban wrapped around her head and a sparkly pin set in it. She wore her new diamond bracelet too. Papa said, "Three of the best-looking women in all of Georgia. And they're all mine—at least for another hour."

Somehow, we all got to the church. Once there, I almost fainted over the size of the crowd. "What happened to your 'little wedding'?" I asked Adel as we peeked through the curtain in the back of the church.

She looked bewildered. "I really don't know."

My heart gave a jump when I saw Jason sitting alone in one of the pews. It hadn't occurred to me that he might come. He was dressed in a suit and looked good enough to make my knees go weak. I silently prayed that I wouldn't trip and make a fool of myself preceding Adel up the aisle.

The church had never looked prettier. Red and white poinsettias adorned the altar area along with a huge Christmas tree off to the side, wreaths at the end of each pew and two white candelabras ablaze with candles. By the time the wedding music started, I was so nervous I thought I was going to throw up. "Don't spoil my wedding," Adel hissed in my ear, ever sympathetic to me.

"Go on, honey," Papa urged more kindly. "We'll be right behind you."

I walked slowly down the aisle, looking straight ahead, my hands so cold I couldn't feel them and my knees knocking. I took my place at the front of the church and watched Sandy, then Adel and Papa, come up the aisle. I had to admit Adel was beautiful, and the look on Barry's face spoke of pure love. Once Papa handed Adel over, he went to sit with Mama. I could see that she was crying. I listened to Adel and Barry say their vows, and before I knew it, the ceremony was over and I was at the back of the church, hugging and congratulating Barry and Adel, and the guests were pouring out the doors.

I missed Becky Sue. I wanted a friend, but only adults swarmed around me. Suddenly I felt a tap on my shoulder, and I turned to face Jason. "You look outstanding," he said.

I felt my face grow warm. "Thank you. I didn't know you were coming. But I'm glad you did."

He said, "Your mother told Carole I should come. So I did."

Someone called me to come back up front for proper photographs.

"I'll see you later," he said.

I could have floated into the picture-taking session. I hoped people would take the smile on my face to mean that I was happy for my sister, which I was, of course. But I was happy for myself also. Not only had the wedding gone perfectly, but Jason had shown up and told me I looked "outstanding." I marveled at how just a simple word from the right person could make me feel like I was glowing from the inside out and walking on clouds at the same time.

# Fifteen

Jason didn't stay at the reception long. I didn't blame him because it was dull as dishwater, but it made me mad because he'd cut out when I'd been looking forward to hanging out with him. I stayed in the fellowship hall because it was required, but just as soon as Adel and Barry fed each other wedding cake, I put on my coat, hitched up my skirt and started walking home. I realized it was a mistake after two blocks in the high heels dyed to match my dress.

The weather grew colder and a wind kicked up, and although I was freezing, I was stewing inside at the same time. Jason could have stuck around to keep me company instead of running off, but he hadn't. I told myself I was stupid to care about him, because he'd never care about me.

Lost in thought, I stepped off a curb and Jason cut across my path with his motorcycle.

"Climb on," he said. "Your face is as blue as your dress."

I teetered between pain and desire. "I've never ridden on a cycle. Not sure I know how."

"Just ease on the back. Keep your legs off the exhaust pipe and put your arms around me."

It took a few tries for me to balance behind him sitting sidesaddle. I linked my arms around him gingerly, determined not to enjoy being so close to him, but the second he kicked off, my arms tightened and I hung on for dear life. The wind whipped through my carefully prepared hair, and despite my chattering teeth, I felt exhilarated. The ride was over in far too short a time. He pulled up in our driveway, parked the cycle at the side of the house and followed me inside. In the entrance hall, he took both my hands in his and rolled them briskly, and soon I could feel warmth creeping into them again. I heard the ticking of the grandfather clock and realized that we were there alone.

His proximity was having quite an effect on me, and I stepped away. "I'll change clothes."

"No." He caught my hand. "Leave the dress on. I like looking at you in it."

Any anger I'd felt toward him evaporated like

water on a hot stove. *He likes me in the dress.* "All right," I said.

"But you might want to fix your hair."

I hurried upstairs and into Adel's room, where I kicked off the heels and slipped on my comfortable clogs. When I looked in the mirror, I almost gagged. My hair looked as if it had been attacked with an eggbeater. I quickly ripped out the pins and arrangement of curls and brushed out the hair spray. I took some deep breaths and told my reflection, "Steady, Darcy. Slow down and act like you couldn't care less that Jason is waiting for you downstairs. Don't make a fool of yourself."

I found Jason in the living room in front of our Christmas tree.

"Here I am," I said, stating the obvious.

He checked me out from head to toe, then grinned. "Better." He walked to the mantel and studied the family pictures set between the evergreen garlands. "Carole says your family has lived in this town for over a hundred years."

"That's the truth." I was glad he'd brought up a topic I knew about. I told him the story about my great-great-grandmother shooting herself a Yankee during the Civil War.

"She killed him?" He seemed impressed.

I jumped in, explaining, "Goodness no. Turned out he was a poor boy cut off from his platoon and foraging for food round the farm. So she felt obliged to nurse him back to health, and when he was well, he felt obliged to marry her— which was just as well, 'cause at the age of twenty-five, Great-great-grandmother was on her way to becoming an old maid. Not that she wasn't pretty—she was. But because there were no mar-rying men left around these parts. Most were off fighting or had died in the war."

He grinned at me and, feeling a rush of em-barrassment, I stopped talking. "Did I say some-thing amusing?"

"No, I just like to hear you talk," he said.

"I know I talk too much. Sorry." I walked to the sofa and sat on the edge of a cushion. "I reckon someone will be here shortly." I almost added "to rescue you."

He sat beside me. "The wedding was good," he said. "I went to Carole and Jim's, but I don't re-member much about it."

An awkward silence settled between us. I lamented my lack of social skills, cursed my in-ability to make small talk in the effortless girly way Adel always did. I was wondering if I could check out a book on the subject from the library when he said, "You want a candy cane?" He pulled one from the pocket of his jacket.

"No thanks." Suddenly it occurred to me that he was probably hungry, since he hadn't remained

at the reception. "You want to stay for supper?"
I asked. "Carole brought over a casserole this
morning so we could all have supper together before Barry, Adel and his folks leave for Atlanta.
Sort of a Christmas dinner without the turkey and
the trimmings."

"I'll stay," he said, taking a bite of the candy.
The aroma of peppermint filled the air. "You have
some shaving cream?"

I gave him a blank stare.

"To decorate Barry's car," he said.

"Yes. Of course. Great idea. I'll go get it." I
started to stand.

"Not yet," he said, urging me to stay seated.
He kept looking at me with his hot green eyes and
sucking on the candy cane. I went gooey inside.
"We can't do the car until Barry gets here with it,"
he added.

*Of course. How stupid of me.*

He reached out and tucked my fine blond hair
behind my ear, and I thought I would melt into a
puddle. I might have too, except that I heard the
front door open and people clump into the front
hall. "Darcy, you home?" Mama called.

I bounded off the sofa and into the hall.
"Right here," I said, breathless. "Jason's here too."

We walked back into the living room together. "Hello, Jason. So glad you're here." Mama
turned to me. "Please help Carole in the kitchen.

Adel's gone up to change, and just as soon as everybody has had a bite to eat, they'll get on the road." She rubbed her temples and I saw that she looked pale.

"You all right?"

"Just a headache. I'm going to lie down till it passes. Long day," she said with an apologetic smile. "But a good one."

Worried about Mama, I said, "I'm on it. Don't worry about a thing."

"I'll help too," Jason offered quickly. "I'm used to my sister ordering me around the kitchen."

Papa came into the room and held out his hand to Mama. "Come on, Joy. Let's get you tucked in for a spell."

"Please give everybody my apologies. And don't let Adel leave without coming up to tell me goodbye," she said over her shoulder as he led her up the stairs.

I watched, feeling scared. "Mama's still not over her hospital stay," I said to Jason, trying to console myself.

He didn't answer, but he looked at me with a whole lot more compassion than I ever expected.

The meal tasted good, but we all felt Mama's absence keenly. Eventually Adel went up to finish packing, and Jason and I drifted out to the car in the driveway with cans of shaving cream. The work went fast because Barry's father and Papa joined in and soon we had the car plastered with Just Married signs, shaving cream hearts and other graffiti suitable for the occasion. When Adel saw it, she gave a shriek, but I could tell she wasn't too bent out of shape. Barry just shook his head and loaded Adel's bag.

"I want to tell Mama goodbye," Adel said to Barry. "I'll be right back."

I hadn't been invited, but I followed her up to Mama's room anyway. The bedroom was lit only by a night-light glowing from a wall socket, and it smelled of Mama's lavender-scented perfume. Her dress lay in an abandoned puddle on the floor.

"Mama?" Adel said softly.

"I'm awake. Come in." Mama pulled herself upright in the bed and turned on the bedside lamp.

"You feeling better?" Adel asked, sitting down on the side of the bed. I stood behind her.

"Better," Mama said.

I saw a cluster of bottles on the small table. I counted five prescription bottles and wondered if they were all for headaches.

"We're leaving," Adel said.

"You have a wonderful honeymoon and a safe trip."

"We'll be back on Monday to take my things to the apartment," Adel said. "I don't know how much time we have left before the army sends us away. I hope it doesn't send us too far," she added, which I thought peculiar. For years, Adel had talked about leaving Conners behind for good. Why was she recanting?

"You'll never be far from my heart," Mama said.

Adel began to cry, and Mama pulled her into her arms. "There, there, baby girl. You go start yourself a wonderful life."

My sister's tears upset me.

"Darcy will be here," Mama said, peering up at me.

I nodded vigorously. "I will. I'll be right here, Adel."

Adel reached for a tissue. She stood, but I could see that she was trembling. "Thank you for my wonderful wedding. I'll never forget it."

She went to the door and I tagged along, because everyone was waiting downstairs with handfuls of rice and birdseed to toss at the bride and groom and I didn't want to miss out. I could tell that Mama wanted to come for the rice-tossing ceremony but that she was hurting. She said, "You give your sister a nice send-off, Darcy, from both of us."

"I can come back after they're gone," I suggested.

"No. Your papa will come up. He'll be with me." She shut her eyes and sank back down into the pillows. "Tell everyone I'm sorry I can't join in today."

Adel said, "They all understand." She had paused at the door. The lamp threw shadows beyond its circle of light. Mama looked wilted and fragile in the bed, like a new flower bud hit by a sudden frost.

"Merry Christmas," Adel said.

"Merry Christmas to both of you," Mama said.

Out in the hallway, Adel took me by the shoulders. "You take care of her, Darcy. You're the one with her now."

"Of course I will," I said. I couldn't understand why Adel's leaving should be so sad for her and Mama. Not that I wouldn't miss my sister. Surely I would! But she'd be coming for visits.

Downstairs we put on our coats and lined up on the sidewalk. Barry and Adel ducked down and ran through our pelting of rice and seed. Barry's folks got into the backseat of the car. The rest of us stood on the lawn and waved goodbye as they drove off, honking the horn. Not long afterward, everybody else left too. Then there was just me and Papa. He went up to be with Mama and I drifted aimlessly about the house before finally going upstairs and changing into my flannel nightgown.

Even though I knew my parents were in their room, I felt like I was all alone. I reviewed scenes of the afternoon—the wedding ceremony, the memory of my arms around Jason, the way he had warmed my hands in his, the sight of my sister telling Mama goodbye, then Adel driving off into another life—all the memories left me unbearably, inexplicably sad. Finally I carried my new portable record player into Adel's room, slipped between the rumpled white sheets and put on my forty-five record of Olivia Newton-John singing "I Honestly Love You." I cried as I listened to it over and over, while sadness soaked through me like summer rain and I fell asleep in my sister's bed.

# Sixteen
## *January*

Becky Sue pumped me for every detail about the wedding. I spilled my guts, even telling her about my ride on Jason's motorcycle. I just left out the personal part: how off-balance I felt whenever I was near him. I saw no need to open *that* can of worms. Soon our discussion turned to the party at Patti's. I personally didn't think Jason would show up, so that took a lot of the anticipation away for me, but Becky was counting on Russell making an appearance, and I was hoping he would for her sake.

On the home front, Mama was feeling better, and on Monday, the day before the big party, Adel and Barry picked up Adel's belongings. They stayed for supper before driving back to Atlanta and their new apartment. Barry was to be on duty during the holiday, but before they left, Mama reminded Adel to cook traditional Southern dishes for New Year's Day—corn bread, greens, hog jowls and black-eyed peas peppered with hot sauce. Eating jowls and peas meant a year of good luck, which all of us needed in facing 1975.

On New Year's Eve, Becky's mother drove us to the party, but Becky asked her to let us off far enough from the cabin that no one would see us arriving by her mother-as-chauffeur service. We needn't have worried. Cars were parked helter-skelter on the dirt road leading to the cabin, and it was pitch dark.

"Are you sure Patti's parents are going to be there?" Mrs. Johnson asked when we got out of the car.

"That's what Patti said," Becky Sue answered with a perfectly straight face.

Patti already had announced to her friends that her folks had other plans that night, but they'd threatened to "drop in" and "check on us," which no one believed for a minute.

"I'll be here to pick you up at twelve-thirty," Becky's mother said, craning her neck and checking out the line of cars. "You're lucky your father's allowing you to come at all. I expect you two to act like adults," she was adding as Becky slammed the car door.

The closer we got to the cabin, the more cars and people we saw. "I think the whole school showed up," Becky said. "I hope I can spot Russell in this crowd."

Word of Patti's party had spread far and wide, because I saw kids I didn't recognize from schools besides ours. Couples were making out in cars, others were sitting on hoods and fenders of cars and one group even had a campfire going on the front lawn. It was still winter and cold that night to boot. But if I thought it was crowded outside the cabin, nothing prepared me for going inside. Becky and I faced wall-to-wall bodies, blaring rock music and gyrating dancers. Furniture had been shoved against the walls and area rugs rolled up. Cigarette smoke hung in the air like swamp fog.

Becky tried to say something to me, but I couldn't hear her above the noise. I pointed to the front door and wiggled my way back outside, where I took in great gulps of fresh air. Already, I wasn't having a good time. Coughing because of the smoke, Becky said, "There's beer in the kitchen."

"I hate beer," I said, amazed that she could have learned that fact in the short time we'd been inside.

"Me too. Maybe there are colas. And rum."

"I don't like rum either."

She knew this was true, because we'd raided her father's liquor cabinet once when we were twelve and sampled every kind of alcohol he owned. With the first couple of sips, I'd felt mellow and giggly. Then I went loopy, and after that I got sick as a dog, and so did Becky. We told our parents it was the stomach flu, but I swore to the Lord then and there that if I lived, I would never drink alcohol again. Baptists had the right idea about steering clear of the "devil's brew," as Pastor Jim called it.

"Let me check around about Russell," she said, and left me shivering on the porch. In fifteen minutes, she was back.

"Find him?" I asked, hugging my arms for warmth.

"He didn't come." She was scowling. "What do you want to do?" She sounded frustrated, as if I was responsible for spoiling her evening.

I was about to suggest calling her mother to come and take us back home where we could eat popcorn and watch TV when two people started yelling at each other on the front lawn. We turned and saw J.T. and Donna standing toe to toe.

"You're cheating on me! Don't deny it!" J.T. hollered.

"Leave me alone. You're drunk as a skunk!" Donna fired back.

J.T. was weaving and bobbing and looked as

threatening as a raging bull. "Not until you tell me who he is!"

Donna turned to walk away, and J.T. grabbed her arm. "Let go of me, J.T."

"Not till you tell me who you're sneaking around with behind my back. No one cheats on me!"

Donna struggled to free her arm. "You're hurting me. Let go."

He shoved her backward. "You're a tramp."

"And you're a pig."

"Not too much of a pig for you to take a Christmas gift from," J.T. barked at her.

"That piece of cheesy crap? It turned my neck green."

I stared openmouthed because anyone could see Donna was flirting with disaster. J.T.'s expression looked wild. "I could choke you!" He grabbed for her neck.

Two of his friends pulled him away, saying, "Settle down, J.T. She ain't worth it."

Donna didn't seem to have the brains God gave a goat because she screeched, "You don't own me, J. T. Rucker! I can do what I want. I can see who I want."

J.T. fought his friends' hold, but he was too drunk to break free. Three of Donna's friends wisely took her arms and dragged her off.

"When I find the bastard, I'll kill him!" J.T. all but screamed after her. "And you'll be responsible. You hear me? His death will be your fault!"

He was shouting at empty air. Everybody outside the cabin stood motionless, watching the scene play out. With a growl, he shook off his friends and staggered toward the porch. "Let me go and get out of my way. I need a beer."

As he lumbered toward the steps, I pulled Becky Sue to the edge of the porch and out of his path. My back brushed the railing and I held my breath. I surely didn't want him seeing me, so certain was I that he'd have something hateful to say about Adel. I was lucky. He didn't notice me and Becky Sue. Instead, he crashed through the front door, knocking people aside and shoving his way through the crowd. I said to Becky, "Let's get out of here."

"Good idea."

We hightailed it down the steps and into the safety of the darkness.

"Wow. What do you suppose brought that on?" Becky asked.

"I wonder if it's true," I said. "I wonder if she's cheating on him."

"Who'd be so stupid? Besides, J.T. and Donna have broken up before. They'll be back together in a week, wait and see." Becky flapped her arms. "I'm freezing."

"Me too, but I think we'd better stay out here."

We eventually found an unoccupied car and climbed inside to stay out of the cold and wait for Becky's mother to show up. Russell never did surface, so the party was a bust and, except for the fracas with Donna and J.T., out of Becky's and my league. Still, I couldn't help wondering if J.T.'s suspicions were founded in truth or in his drunken imagination. Not that it mattered. If Donna could make J.T. suffer, then more power to her.

In January, President Ford extended his earlier offer of clemency to Vietnam draft dodgers. This made plenty of people in our part of Georgia pretty darn mad. There was a time when I wouldn't have noticed such things, but ever since Barry had become a part of our family, I kept myself up on world events. I read editorials in Conners' weekly *Herald-News*, which didn't usually print much more than ball scores and reports about town meetings and social affairs. However, they gave a nice big write-up to Adel's wedding, which pleased Mama no end.

Still, I quickly learned that if I wanted real news, I had to go to the public library and read papers from other parts of the country—*The New York Times*, the *Atlanta Journal*, the *Chicago*

*Tribune* and even *The Daily News* from Washington, D.C. I compared stories and opinions and there was no doubt about it—the South was a whole lot angrier about the clemency offer than other places.

Also in January, the province of Phuoc Long in South Vietnam fell to North Vietnam, which upset folks in our area even more because that meant that the Communists were encroaching farther south and that South Vietnam was losing the war. I think that to some in Conners, it was a little like Sherman invading Georgia in the Civil War. At least that's what Papa said whenever he returned from the barbershop or the hardware store, where he'd discuss these things with other men from our town.

I spent hours going over Kyle's scrapbook about his tour of duty. The photographs and his journal entries told stories that both touched my heart and horrified me.

*January 21, 1968: Khe Sanh military base, after midnight, NVA artillery scored a direct hit on our ammunition stores. Explosions keep going off. It's like the whole world is burning down around us.*

*January–February 1968: We're busiest after dark when the NVA is most active. We need supplies, over 160 tons a day, just to keep fighting.*

*February 11: Lost a C-130 Hercules Transport that was trying to land and bring us supplies. Entire crew dead.*

*February '68: The enemy shells us every day. At night we sleep in shifts. By day we dig trenches, fill sandbags and improve our bunkers. Trenches are knee-deep in mud. I've got foot rot because my feet are always wet. Food scarce. Two C rations per day. Rats everywhere. Frank shot one crawling on his sleeping bag and blew off part of his own foot—a mistake, but it got him out of here. Casualties daily. No mail, no nothing. Dear God, I'd give all my worldly goods for a hot shower and a clean bed.*

*Choppers being sent in with supplies now. The supply choppers are preceded by Sky Hawk fighters and Huey gunships and they're in and out in five minutes. The sweet sounds of those helicopters are the highlight of my day. I watch them swirl down, throwing winds that make trees sway and break. They take the wounded, leave supplies. The choppers rise up like great dark angels, taking my dreams of escape from this hellhole with them.*

*We got pinned down today near hill 861 in a firefight. Snipers hid in trees and began to pick us off. Longest night of my life. Teddy Bryant, next to me, took one in the chest. I talked to him all night long to keep him awake, and when the choppers came to rescue us I carried him on my back to the belly of the transport. A useless waste of energy, according to the medic. Teddy was already dead.*

*March '68: Dysentery and sores are driving me insane. Three more of my buddies are dead from enemy fire.*

*June '68: After a 77-day siege and hundreds of marines KIA (killed in action), the base at Khe Sanh was abandoned and blown up today by our own troops because Washington's decided it's no longer militarily strategic to remain there. So many died here, and now we're told the place doesn't matter anymore.*

*I have survived when so many of my buddies have not. I don't know why. Maybe to tell people that I have seen Hell and felt its fiery brimstone, and that it is a place where no one should ever have to go.*

I cried when I read Kyle's journal. I saw the scenes he described, felt his anguish over losing his friends. I got mad at our President and Congress because they had allowed the fighting to go on for so long. With five months of school remaining, I kept tweaking and embellishing the chart with photos I cut from *Life* and *Look* and *Time* magazines. I knew the names of the military helicopters and fighter jets, the names of the battles, the locations of the crucial cities. Yes, I was becoming a real expert on the war in Vietnam.

Then, in the last week of January, two things

happened that put everything else out of my mind. Adel called to say that Barry and she were moving to Germany, courtesy of the U.S. Army. And my mother returned to the hospital for more chemotherapy.

# Seventeen
## *February*

⁂

With Mama back in the hospital in Atlanta and Adel gone to Germany, I faced coming home to our empty house every day after school. I hated it. The house I'd grown up in seemed wintry and dark, a shell sucked clean of life. The gardens were barren, with leafless bushes and brown grass and birds not yet returning to build nests or sing their sweet songs. Papa didn't come home until after six, sometimes later. "Tax season is on us," he told me. "These next three months are the busiest of the year, so you'll be on your own a lot, Darcy. Can you handle it?"

Naturally I said yes. I made a stab at cooking and discovered that cooking and timing delivery to the table were much harder than I'd imagined. However, Mama's prayer circle from church still brought over casseroles, so Papa and I ate regularly. I did my homework. I watched some television. I went to bed. My life became colorless and drab.

On weekends, Papa and I went to visit Mama. She suffered terribly. She was worn down by chemo and ravaged by cancer; I could hardly bear to look at her. If I had thought her first chemo treatments were awful, these were downright horrific. Mama again lost her hair, including eyebrows and eyelashes. She said, "I look like a plucked chicken." She had terrible sores inside her mouth, making it impossible for her to eat or drink. She was racked by nausea and lost so much weight that she became just skin and bones. Fear lived inside my heart like a worm in an apple. "She's not getting better," I told Papa after every visit.

"She will," he said. "Like last time, she'll get better and come home to us."

I told Becky Sue, "The chemo is poisoning my mother."

Becky Sue let me rant and rail and patted my shoulder and told me to pray harder. I hesitated to tell her that I'd given up on prayer because God wasn't listening. If he had been, then my mama would have been getting well and would have come home and stayed home. I swore off Sunday school and sat in the far back pews with Papa during church services. I attended youth group, but only for Becky's sake. I just couldn't feel anything but resentment toward God.

It was Becky who signed us up at school for the Valentine dance's decoration committee.

"Why'd you do that?" I asked as she dragged me to the gym for the first meeting.

"Because it's the only dance of the year for the whole high school. Because dressy clothes are mandatory and therefore everybody looks their best. Because you need to think about something else for a change. Because it might actually be fun." She ticked off the reasons on her fingers as she spoke.

"Oh, sure. Cutting out paper hearts and making red-and-white paper chains is so much fun."

"Don't be so crabby. I mean, what else have you got to do?"

She was right about that. It wasn't as if my life was full. I'd given up on Jason—a secret crush that would never amount to anything. He usually acknowledged me when I saw him in the halls, but he'd stopped coming to teen group at church, and no amount of begging him to return, according to Carole, persuaded him to do so. I considered Becky's suggestion.

"Oh, all right," I said grudgingly. "I'll be on the committee with you."

Our gym teacher, Mrs. Poston, supervised the plans for the dance, making sure we had the proper supplies and a scheme for decorating. Of course, I had no plans to *attend* the dance, because except for Jason, there wasn't a boy in our school I'd go with, even if someone asked me—which no one would—but Becky held out hope that Russell would ask her. Three days before the big dance in the gym, Russell surprised us both by doing so. I'd heard that his first choice, Susan Wilson, had turned him down, but I saw no reason to puncture Becky Sue's balloon with that kind of news.

"You have to come," she told me the day we were hanging decorations around the gym. The dance was to start at seven and we only had a few hours to get the work done, so the committee had excused absences for that Friday afternoon.

"I don't want to come," I told Becky. "Why should I?"

"To support me."

"You've got Russell to support you."

"But he's a guy and you're my best friend. Who'll go to the bathroom with me?"

I rolled my eyes. "I imagine you can pee by yourself."

"That's not what I mean and you know it. I *need* you there. What if Russell and I don't hit it off?"

"You've been talking about Russell Danby all year. And now, at the eleventh hour, you're afraid you might not get along with him?" I wanted to take my best friend by the shoulders and shake her. "I don't want to go!" I exclaimed. "I'll stand out like a sore thumb."

"Lots of others will be coming stag," Becky insisted. "You won't be alone." She leaned closer to me. "I've heard that Donna won't be going with J.T. Don't you want to see who she comes with?"

"They haven't made up yet?"

"Not even speaking," Becky said smugly.

I admitted that I was curious, but other things had occupied my mind in the past month. I told Becky Sue, "No way am I coming to the dance."

But in the end, she won out.

When I arrived home from school on Friday and read a note from Papa saying that he'd be working late, and when I saw the long, lonely Friday night stretching out in front of me like an eternity, I knew I couldn't stay there by myself. I hurried upstairs and called Mrs. Poston and told her that I'd be glad to man the punch bowl and take care of the table throughout the evening. She volunteered to pick me up early, for which I was grateful, because that meant I could arrive early with her and wouldn't have to walk into the gym for all the world to see that I was utterly and totally alone.

I pulled my bridesmaid dress from the closet and made a stab at dabbing on makeup leftovers from Adel, but could only brush my hair and let it hang to my shoulders in its usual style. "Who cares?" I told my reflection in the mirror. No one would be looking at me.

The gym filled quickly with couples, and with the lights dimmed and a disco ball scattering sparkles every which way and the walls decorated with giant hearts, cupids and paper doilies, the place looked pretty good. Terri Hanson's older brother set up a DJ corner and played stacks of records, one right after the other. I took my place behind the punch table and poured red punch into plastic cups for all who asked. And I saw that Becky Sue had been correct when she'd predicted that many kids would come stag. A whole line of chairs along the west wall was filled with girls and guys all dressed in their party best and trying hard to look bored and uninterested in each other.

"You're here!" Becky squealed the minute she saw me. She was dressed in a long pink dress with pretty, puffy long sleeves and ribbons. She wore a wrist corsage.

"I couldn't let my best friend pee alone," I said, handing her a cup of punch. "Of course, your kidneys will have to coordinate with my breaks."

She leaned closer. "Russell is wonderful. His eyes lit up like Christmas tree bulbs when I came down the stairs."

I was happy for Becky, but envious too. It might be nice to have some boy make a fuss over me. "Go dance," I told her. "And don't get lip-stick on his collar."

She walked off in a flounce of taffeta, and Russell met her on the dance floor. I watched them snuggle amid all the other couples. I poured another cup of punch and looked up to see J.T. holding out his hand. "If I'd known you were go-ing to be here unattached, I'd have dumped my plans, fallen at your feet and begged you to be my date," he taunted.

I scanned the room as if searching for some-one. "So who did you pay to come with you?"

He sneered at me. "I'm with JoAnn Moser. And she volunteered."

"What—no Donna?" I was pushing my luck but didn't much care because he had made me mad with his teasing.

His expression grew stony and I knew my barb had hit home. "She's dog food. Who needs her?"

"Jason," I whispered, shocked. For there he was, just walking in the door, holding Donna's hand.

J.T. turned, and although I couldn't see his face, I did see his back straighten and his big, beefy hand clench into a fist.

Jason was dressed in jeans, but also a sport coat and white shirt. Donna wore soft yellow and her smile looked radiant. Suddenly, all became clear to me. It was Jason whom Donna had been seeing secretly. It was Jason who had broken J.T.'s hold on his longtime girlfriend. And by coming to the dance together, they were flaunting it to every teen in Conners. J.T., the mighty football god, had been snaked by an outsider, a nobody, a motorcycle-riding hood and a Yankee. I would have laughed out loud if my own heart hadn't been broken.

Principal Hagan and the coach materialized as if from thin air. Their presence meant there would be no problems at the dance. I picked up the cup of punch J.T. had set on the table. "Don't you want your punch, J.T.?" I asked sweetly. "Have you lost your taste for it?"

He shot me a withering look. "Stuff it, Quinlin." He lumbered off, found JoAnn and half dragged her to the door. Everyone heard them arguing about leaving so early, but in the end J.T. got his way. As he usually did.

Once they were gone, the floor filled up again with couples, and music filled the gym. I hardly heard anything. My hands were shaking so badly that I spilled punch on the table and had to find paper towels to sop up the mess. I didn't care. All I wanted was to leave. I started making up a story in my head for Mrs. Poston to excuse myself when Becky Sue came up and said, "Time for a break."

I left my duties without a backward glance and followed her into the girls' room, crammed with chattering females crowded around the mirror. "What's up?" Becky asked once we'd carved out a space for ourselves. "You're pale as a ghost."

"J.T. was hateful to me," I said. The half-truth was my protective shield.

"Well, he certainly got slapped down tonight," Becky said with a note of satisfaction. "Donna really embarrassed him. I didn't think the old girl had it in her, but I'm glad she did."

A senior and one of Donna's girlfriends, overhearing our conversation, said, "Donna's been sneaking around with Jason since Christmas. At first she was just using him to get back at J.T., 'cause he's so mean to her. But the little mouse got caught in her own snare. Now she's crazy about Jason."

I could have lived forever without hearing that, but I carefully hid my feelings behind a mask of indifference. Becky Sue hung on her every word. "J.T. won't like being crossed," she said. "Did Donna think about the consequences?"

The girl shrugged. "Jason knows he's playing with fire, but he doesn't seem to care. It's sort of romantic if you think about it, having two guys squabbling over you."

I didn't want to think about it.

Once we were back in the gym, Becky again asked me, "Are you sure you're okay? You're not acting like yourself."

"I told you I didn't want to come to this dance," I said. "I should have stayed home."

Becky Sue gave me a hug. "Tomorrow night we'll have a sleepover."

"I'm going with Papa to visit Mama."

"Soon as you get home, you come over."

"What if Russell wants you to go out with him?"

"Why, he can just wait. Goodness, I've waited long enough for him."

Knowing she was trying to cheer me up, I forced a smile. By then many of the couples were leaving and the dance was winding down. I was almost back to my post behind the punch table when Jason stepped in front of me. "Can we dance?" he asked.

"Where's your date? Chasing after J.T.?" I felt mean-spirited and humiliated too because he'd trampled on my tender feelings for him.

"Donna's sitting this one out."

I glanced around and saw her perched on a stag-line chair. She was giving both of us dagger looks.

"What is she? A trained puppy? Waiting for you to snap your fingers?"

"Ouch," he said mildly. "Why so hostile?"

"I'm busy," I said, stepping around him.

"But I want to dance with you." He stepped into my path.

"Well, did it occur to you that I might not want to dance with you?" My heart was hammering like a drum.

He looked down at me, grinned and took me in his arms. "It never crossed my mind."

And at that moment, the DJ put on "I Honestly Love You." My breath caught. I looked into Jason's face and saw only softness. "Dance with me," he whispered.

If I had been butter, I would have melted.

His embrace tightened, and with my body fitted to his, we moved as one to the music. I felt the heat of his skin on mine, the warmth of his breath on my cheek. His lips pressed against my hair. The words of the song wrapped around me like fine ribbons, binding me to Jason. He didn't know—could never know—how much I wanted to be near him this way. "*I love you; I honestly love you. . . .*" The voice on the record and the one in my head flowed into one pure stream. I struggled not to cry. *It's a song, just a song,* I told myself. It meant nothing and this dance meant nothing.

When the music ended, Jason slowly untangled from our embrace. He stared down at me, his green eyes serious, his delicious mouth inches from mine. "You are beautiful, Darcy Quinlin."

I shook my head, not trusting my voice.

"Then believe this—you're worth two of girls like Donna."

But Donna was with him and I wasn't.

He raised my hand to his lips and, like a cavalier from an old storybook, kissed it. "Thank you for the dance," he said, and walked away.

Tears stung my eyes, but I didn't look back to see him leave with Donna. For that was more pain than I could bear. I made it home before I broke down, and there alone on my bed in the moonlight, I told myself that I was being foolish and stupid to spill my tears over a love I should not feel for a boy I could not have.

# Eighteen
## *March*

In the last week of February, I noticed that the daffodils were poking their heads through the soil. Just seeing their bright yellow faces gave me a thrill. Everywhere I looked in our backyard, spring was announcing its arrival. Lacy yellow fringe lined the branches of the forsythia bushes, and the azalea bushes were bursting into vibrant shades of orange, fuchsia, purple and lilac. I saw tiny tight buds on the dogwood trees and a mantle of purple phlox beginning to edge over the stone walls by the pond. Soon the iris beds would be in bloom. It made me happy, knowing that Mama would come home to find her gardens ablaze with color and new growth. I made a note on the calendar to pull up the pansies and remulch the beds. Once the irises were spent, I would plant begonias, geraniums and verbena in the sunny beds, impatiens and petunias in the shady ones.

Friday, March 1, was a teachers' work day and we had no school. By noon, the air was warm enough to go without a sweater. Eager to hurry spring along, I headed off to the nursery, pulling the wagon Mama sometimes used to transport flowerpots and flats of annuals around the yard. The walk there was a long one, but I felt like making the trip on foot just so I could smell the air and feel the sunshine on my bare arms.

I decided to cut across near the junkyard on the edge of town, run-down and overgrown with weeds and deserted except for a few crumbling buildings. I rounded the corner of one shuttered building and stopped stock-still. Less than twenty yards away, Jason was riding in lazy circles on his motorcycle. When he saw me, he gunned the engine, stood the machine upright on its back wheel and, once it bounced back to the ground, drove toward me. He slid to a stop, kicking up gravel. "Hello, Darcy. What are you doing out here?"

"Walking," I said. He looked good enough to make my insides turn into buttercream. We hadn't had any contact since the dance.

"Pretty lonely place to be walking by yourself."

"Are you thinking about my safety? This is Conners, not Chicago."

"You look like a little kid pulling your little wagon."

I was in no mood to be teased. "I'm buying flowers up at the nursery. Some of us have things to do."

He grinned. "Hey, I'm busy. I'm practicing tricks on my cycle. Not much else to do around this excuse for a town."

"Sorry you're so bored." I jerked the wagon to the left of him. He caught my arm as I passed.

"Why are you mad at me?" he asked.

There was no way I could tell him that my anger was rooted in frustration. That it was easier to dislike him than it was to long for him so much that it made me ache. "I'm not mad at you. I just have things to do." I began walking, the wagon clattering behind me on the rough ground.

He dismounted and walked alongside me. "I rode past your house last weekend. I was going to say hello, but you weren't home."

"We visit Mama every Saturday at the hospital."

"How's she doing?"

I didn't get to answer because just then we heard the roar of an engine and turned to see J.T.'s truck bearing down on us. Jason grabbed my arm and pulled me aside just as the truck skidded to a halt. J.T. and his friend Frankie were out of the cab in a split second and standing like a wall in front of us.

"Well, what have we here?" J.T. said, glaring at us. "If it isn't Darcy Quinlin and her good buddy Motorcycle Creep."

Fear welled up inside me. Not for myself, because I didn't believe J.T. would harm me, but fear for Jason. "You go on, J.T.," I said. "No one's bothering you."

"You hear that, Frankie? She wants us to go away." The sneer on J.T.'s face was frightening. "You stay and watch, Darcy. I want you to see what we do to him."

"I don't want any trouble," Jason said.

"Well, you've got it," J.T. said, balling his fists and taking a step closer. "I don't like someone taking what belongs to me. And I *really* don't like you."

Of course he was referring to Donna—as if she was a piece of property instead of a person. I thought about screaming for help, but my tongue felt like a swollen blob in my mouth. And out here, we were alone. There was no one to hear me no matter how loudly I screamed.

Jason pulled me behind him as Frankie closed in on our left.

What happened next was so quick that it blurred. One second Jason was shielding me, the next he was crouched with an open switchblade in his hand. He lunged sideways, caught the fabric of Frankie's shirt with the tip of the blade and drew it clear across his stomach, slicing open the shirt. Frankie yelped and staggered. He stumbled and fell. My stomach heaved, for I was certain that Jason had stabbed him and he was dead. J.T. stopped advancing. The blade of the knife flashed in the sun.

"Don't make me cut you," Jason said quietly. He flicked his wrist, made small threatening circles with the blade, then jabbed at the air between him and J.T.

"Hold on, man," J.T. said. He stepped back, tripped over Frankie and landed in a heap on top of him. Both of them lay still, staring up at the shining knife.

Jason stood over them, tossing the knife expertly from one hand to the other. "You stay clear of me, Rucker." Jason's voice was stony cold. "Because if I have to cut you, I'll make certain you never play football again. And as for Donna, you can have her back. I'm through with her."

Nothing moved, not even the air. I stared down at Frankie's slashed shirt. A drop of blood wet the fabric, and I realized that although the shirt had been slit across the entire front of Frankie's body, Jason had left only one small nick

in the skin. He could make good on his threat to
J.T., and we all knew it.

Jason caught my hand. "Come on, Darcy. I'll
give you a ride. You can get the wagon later."

We backed toward the cycle and got on. This
time, I wasn't wearing a dress to encumber me. I
straddled the seat behind him, locked my arms
around his waist and clung to him. He kick-
started the engine and roared out of the field,
leaving a cloud of dust and a terrified J. T. Rucker
behind us.

We rode south out of town for miles. I felt icy
cold with the wind whipping around me, my mind
reeling over what I'd seen. When Jason finally
slowed and stopped, we were on a two-lane road
far out in the country. Cows, grazing in a field beside us, gave us curious stares. Jason asked, "You
all right?"

"I—I think so." But I wasn't. I felt shell-
shocked, the way Kyle had described it in his journal. *Numb, with a buzzing in my ears, my skin
prickling all over.*

"You look cold." Jason removed his leather
jacket and slipped it around my shoulders. He
caught the collar on either side in his hands and
pulled me toward him so that I was standing on
tiptoe and only inches from his face. "It's okay,
Darcy. J.T. and I have been on a collision course

for a long time. I'm sorry you had to be there for the crash."

I looked into the depths of his eyes, searching for remorse, or perhaps regret. "Would you have hurt him?"

His expression was resolute. "Yes. I would have hurt him. Because if I didn't, one day he'd hurt me. It's the law of the streets."

"Even in Conners?"

He nodded ruefully. "Even in Conners."

"And are you really throwing Donna back to him?"

"Yes."

"Why?"

"I'm through with her," he said simply. "I never really wanted her."

"Why did you take her from J.T. if you didn't want her?"

Jason shrugged. "Because I could," he said, as if it was the most logical explanation in the world.

His answer left me colder than had the ride through the March air. "Will you take me home?"

He slowly let go of the jacket's collar and stepped aside, putting distance between us that felt as wide as a canyon to me. "Sure," he said. "Let's go."

I got on the cycle and we returned to Conners and my driveway, where I dismounted, handed him his jacket and hurried into my house without so much as telling him thank you, or even goodbye.

Papa had arranged with the hospital for our family to take a phone call from Adel all the way from Germany on the first Saturday in March. Mama, Papa and I were in a small conference room staring at a speakerphone, which was nothing more than a little box sitting beside a telephone on the table. When the phone rang, we all jumped. Papa picked up the receiver, then pushed the button on the speaker box so that we all could hear Adel.

"Mama, I miss you so much" were her first words.

"I miss you too, honey," Mama said.

"How about me, Adel? Do you miss me?" I asked.

"Yes, Darcy. I miss you and Papa both. You still doing good in school?"

"All A's," I said, which was the truth.

"I—I would have never believed I would be so lonesome." Adel sounded weepy.

"It will pass as you adjust. Promise," Mama told her.

"What's it like in Germany?" Papa asked, changing the subject.

"Not like living in Georgia," Adel said. "Barry took me to see the Berlin Wall and it was scary.

The East German border patrol walks along the top with machine guns and they pick off anybody who tries to escape from their side of Berlin. Someone got shot last night trying to cross the border."

"That's awful," Mama said. I saw her take Papa's hand. "Adel, why are you crying?"

"B-because I'm so lonely. I—I want to come home."

I thought, *Adel wants to come back to Conners? Adel, who couldn't wait to shake the dust of our small Southern town off her dainty little feet?* "But why?" I asked. "You've always wanted to travel."

Papa gave me a glance that warned I shouldn't digress. "How's Barry doing?" Papa asked. "Does he know how you feel?"

"Barry's wonderful. It's just that he's gone a lot. We hardly ever see each other. We live in horrible housing. It's always cold and the kitchen's about the size of my closet back home."

"Aren't there other army wives in the same boat?" Papa asked.

"I really don't like them all that much. They're different from me. Army life is—is . . ." She searched for words and finally settled on "I just don't like it here. I want to come home."

"But, honey, you're married," Mama said. "Your place is with your husband."

I couldn't believe that Adel was saying the things she was saying.

"Mama, I have something else to tell all of you." Adel's sniffly voice crackled through the speaker box.

"Tell us, honey."

"Mama, I'm going to have a baby. I just found out yesterday."

The three of us sitting at the table looked at each other. Papa's eyebrows shot up, Mama shrugged and I groaned, remembering J.T.'s hateful take on Adel's sudden marriage plans. After a few seconds Mama said, "Why, Adel, honey, that's wonderful news. When?"

"Early November," she said. "The army doctor says I'm just barely six weeks along."

I did a quick calculation and breathed a quiet a sigh of relief. November was eight months away. Adel hadn't been pregnant when she married at Christmastime. "That's so cool!" I blurted out. "I'm going to be an aunt!"

Adel burst into tears. "I'm sick to my stomach every day."

"It's morning sickness. Trust me, it'll pass," Mama said.

"And you're sick, Mama. I can't stand the idea of you so sick with cancer and me so far away."

I was suddenly sympathetic to my sister, which I had not been up to that point. Being worried about Mama's health was something we certainly had in common.

"I'm almost finished with this round of chemo," Mama said. "Then I'll be going back home. So don't worry about me. You just take care of yourself and our grandchild."

We could hear Adel sniffing.

I saw bright tears in Mama's eyes. I felt moisture in my own.

"You take it easy, little girl," Papa said into the speaker. "I don't know how many crying women I can handle at one time."

We all laughed self-consciously, which broke the tension.

"I—I have to go," Adel said. "The communications sergeant who's letting me make this call is saying my time's up."

"I'm glad we talked," Mama said. "And I'm excited and pleased about your news. Give Barry a hug from us."

"I want you to see my baby, Mama," Adel said fiercely. "I want you to hold it in your arms."

"And so do I," Mama said. "You write us, you hear?"

"I'll write every day."

We said our goodbyes, then sat quietly in the room. It had never occurred to me that Mama wouldn't hold the baby when Adel and Barry returned to the States. Yet Adel's pleas had sent a chill through me that made me shiver. I gave my parents a sidelong glance, studying their entwined fingers. Well, of course Mama would see the baby. Her doctors were sending her home, and they wouldn't do that unless she was better. Would they?

# Nineteen

On Monday morning, I was called down to Principal Hagan's office. I knocked on the door, and when he opened it and I walked into the room, I found myself facing Jason, J.T. and Frankie, all sitting in a row of chairs. My mouth went bone-dry.

"Hello, Darcy," Mr. Hagan said. "Sit down and join us."

I sat in the chair he pointed to, across from the three boys.

The principal rocked back on his heels. "First off, Darcy, you're not in any trouble."

I felt no relief.

"I asked you here in hopes that you can clear up some confusion in the story two of these boys are telling me." He gestured toward the stony-faced threesome. "Mr. Rucker and his friend have accused Mr. Polwalski of pulling a knife on them and threatening them with serious bodily harm. In fact"—Mr. Hagan paused, reached for a bag on his desk, opened it and pulled out Frankie's slashed shirt—"they have even brought me evidence to support their story."

I understood the situation instantly. J.T. was getting back at Jason the only way he could—by telling on him.

Mr. Hagan crossed his arms and continued in his strongly accented Southern voice. "Now, I pride myself in knowing what goes on in the lives of my students. Why, I've known most of the kids here all their lives. So, it has not escaped me that Mr. Rucker has, on occasion, given Mr. Polwalski a hard time."

J.T. opened his mouth as if to speak, but Mr. Hagan gave him a withering look. "I am still talking, son." He turned to me. "J.T. says that you were present when this knife incident happened. Therefore, I have called you in to either verify or refute the story."

"What did Jason say?" I asked, buying myself some time.

Mr. Hagan glanced over at Jason, whose expression was inscrutable. "Mr. Polwalski has neither confirmed nor denied the story. In fact, he has said nothing in his defense. Not a word."

Jason's face was a mask of calm, and I

wondered if his silence was peculiar to the streets where he'd grown up. I reminded myself that J.T. and Frankie had been out to do Jason bodily harm. If they hadn't, the knife might never have appeared.

"Darcy?" Mr. Hagan's voice sliced through my thoughts. "Were you present when this alleged incident occurred?"

I nodded.

"And did Mr. Polwalski draw a knife?"

My conscience dogged me to be truthful. And then there *was* my blushing problem—any hint of a lie was likely to turn me cherry red. J.T. shot me threatening looks. Yet what he was doing to Jason angered me. He was a rat fink. He had gone to Principal Hagan because he couldn't get even with Jason any other way. This incident would surely mean an automatic expulsion. And with it, J.T. would be free to strut and brag about how he had gotten Jason thrown out of school. Jason would not graduate, and J.T. would be free to terrorize again. He was a football hero. He was a god. Who would stop him?

I looked up into Mr. Hagan's eyes. "Here's what happened," I said. "J.T. and Frankie were intent on taking Jason out. They found him alone in the junkyard with me and figured it would be a good time to do it. Jason saw them coming. He grabbed my hand and we ran to his motorcycle, got on and got out of there as fast as we could."

J.T. shot forward. "You lying little b—"

"Hush your mouth, J.T.!" Mr. Hagan roared. "You will not speak like that to anyone in my office. Understand?"

"But she's lying! Jason had a knife. You've got the shirt to prove it."

"Anyone could have cut this shirt, J.T.," Mr. Hagan said. He turned back to me. "So, Darcy, you're saying that you never saw a knife?"

I sat very straight, my gaze riveted on the wall just above J.T.'s head. "No, sir, I didn't see a knife." I didn't flinch. And for the first time in the history of my life, my face didn't turn red and betray me.

"But he—" J.T. started.

"You are excused," Mr. Hagan said. "All of you are excused. Return to your classes."

We shuffled to our feet and crossed single file to the door.

"Thank you, Darcy," Mr. Hagan said. "Please give my regards to your mother."

"I will, sir," I said.

In the hall, J.T. brushed past me and might have shoved me into the wall except that Jason sidled between us. We fell into step together.

Jason said, "Hear me, Rucker. If you come back on Darcy in any way, I will hunt you down and finish what I started."

"Are you threatening me again?" J.T. snarled.

"No," Jason said. "I am predicting the future."

J.T. and Frankie kept moving. With a thrill of satisfaction, I watched them swagger down the hall. Without another word, Jason took my hand and ducked out a side door, pulling me with him. The sun shone, but a cool breeze had kicked up.

"I have to go back to class," I said. The enormity of what I'd just done was starting to sink in. I had lied. I had lied to the principal of the school. I, Darcy Rebecca Quinlin, who had been taught from infancy that lying was a sin.

Jason backed me against a brick wall. "Why did you do it, Darcy? Why did you lie for me?" His expression was wary and not one bit grateful.

I raised my chin in defiance. "Don't be so conceited. It wasn't all about you. I saw a chance to slam J.T. He had it coming."

Jason studied my face as if looking for magic writing to appear and give him a message. After a long time, he said, "Thank you for saying what you did. I'm not sorry about what happened, but I wouldn't want to make trouble for Carole and Jim."

"Me either," I said. And of course, I could never tell him that the real reason I had lied was because I loved him. No. I could never tell him that.

Mama came home in the middle of March. The night before Papa was to pick her up, I was writing a paper for English lit class at the kitchen table. Papa pulled out a chair across from me and said, "We need to talk, Darcy."

"All right." I put down my pencil and closed my Shakespeare book.

"Things will be different this time for your mother."

"How so?"

He laced his fingers together. "Dr. Keller will be taking over her care."

This surprised me, for I remembered that the reason she'd gone to Atlanta in the first place was because Dr. Keller couldn't take care of her. "He has new equipment?" I asked.

"No, that's not the kind of care she'll need. The doctors in Atlanta have done all for her that they can. Dr. Keller will be taking over her physical care, the day-to-day things."

I must have looked confused because Papa added, "That is to say, Dr. Keller will make certain that she's pain-free as much as possible."

This made sense. Doc Keller was a whole lot closer than the doctors at Emory. "Okay," I said. "How's he going to do that?"

"There'll be pills, of course, but injections too."

I leaned back in my chair. "Shots for pain?" I said, for clarification. "Faster than pills, I guess."

"I must work. And you must attend school. Therefore, your mother will be spending a large portion of her day here alone at the house. Friends have promised to check in on her. Carole says she'll come every day and fix lunch. I'm having the phone company install another phone line on Monday in our bedroom. If your mother has a bad spell with the pain and nobody's here, she can call Doc Keller herself. If you're here with her, you call Keller."

I nodded, realizing that Papa was giving me an important mission. "You know I will, Papa. I mean, if Mama's hurting, I'll call the doctor to come help without you telling me to."

Papa's brow furrowed and I saw that his eyes were glistening. Concern squeezed my heart; sympathy caused a lump to rise in my throat. I rarely saw my father show emotion.

"What's different this time?" I asked the question, scared of the answer.

"The cancer's moved into her bones, Darcy."

"What about all that chemo she's been having?"

"It helped some. Not enough."

"So that means her pain's going to be a whole lot worse, is that it?"

He gave me a long, sad look. "Yes. It'll be worse."

"Then don't you worry, I'll call Dr. Keller," I told him, hoping to make him more confident about my being alone with Mama if she had a spell of serious pain. "Papa, together we'll help her through this."

He just sat there staring at me until I began to wonder if I'd missed something. Finally, he heaved himself up from the table, came around and touched my cheek. "Course we will. Now, you go on back to your studying and I'm going to the living room to read the paper. When I bring your mother home tomorrow, I'll put her straight to bed and you and I will care for her."

I offered up my sunniest smile because he looked so sad. "To tomorrow," I said, giving him a thumbs-up.

He kissed my forehead and left the kitchen, and I went back to my writing assignment.

Once Mama was home, school and what happened there became less important to me. But the rumors about Jason going after J.T. with a switchblade "for no reason at all" haunted the halls and refused to die. I simply listened when Becky Sue repeated them.

"Everyone's saying that Jason almost stabbed Frankie to death and that nothing's going to be done about it because J.T. has no reliable witnesses," Becky said to me while we were walking home one afternoon in late March.

"That's a problem," I mumbled, acting bored and uninterested. The only part of the stories going around that I knew to be truthful was that Jason and Donna were history.

"Aren't you the quiet one?" Becky Sue gave me one of her practiced looks that said she believed I was saying less than I knew.

"No use adding fuel to the fire," I told her. I changed the subject. "How are you and Russell getting on?"

"Russell and I are doing just fine. He's coming over later to do homework with me."

"He kiss you yet?"

"Don't you think I'd tell you if he had? I don't keep secrets from my best friend," she added pointedly.

I felt a stab of guilt. "Are you saying that I do?"

"I'm not saying any such thing. I'm just making an observation."

"Based on what?"

"Maybe someone saw you getting off Jason's motorcycle on that Friday J.T. said he was attacked. And maybe she's been waiting for weeks for you to tell her about it."

I felt my infamous blush spreading across my cheeks. "He gave me a ride," I said, staring straight ahead. "I was on my way to the nursery when he saw me. And by then I was tired and so he offered me a ride home. That's all there was to it."

"And you didn't see fit to tell me? Your best friend?" She sounded hurt.

"I—I forgot." I winced as I lied.

Becky let out an exaggerated sigh. "Just so you know, it was my dad who found your wagon over by the junkyard and brought it home for you."

I stopped. I had forgotten about the wagon appearing mysteriously on the front porch. I had guessed that Jason had returned it.

"Actually, Dad brought it to our house first," Becky said. "I recognized it as your mother's and told him so. Neither of us could figure out how it had wandered clear across town. I sure hope no one was trying to steal it."

I knew she was waiting for an explanation and I was trying hard to think of one when we turned the corner of my street. Suddenly everything went out of my head, because parked in our driveway was a stranger's car.

"Later!" I called to Becky, and I set off running.

# Twenty

❧ ❧

I slammed into the house and bolted up the stairs. Dr. Keller met me at the top. "Whoa. Slow down, missy," he said.

"But Mama—" My breath was coming in gasps.

"Is sleeping," Dr. Keller said. "She called me and I came over and gave her a shot."

"I want to see her." I tried to go around him, but he took me by the shoulders.

"Let her rest for now. Come down to the kitchen with me and pour me a glass of tea. Please," he added when I didn't budge.

In the kitchen, I opened a tray of ice and put several cubes in a glass. Dr. Keller set his black medical bag on the table. I dragged Mama's cut crystal pitcher from the refrigerator and poured tea into the glass of ice and set it in front of him. "There," I said.

"Thank you." He drained the glass. "Why don't you sit here with me?"

"You sure Mama's all right?"

"The medicine's very powerful. It knocks her out."

I sat, taking deep breaths to calm my trembling. "Papa said you'd come whenever she called. I just wasn't expecting it to be so soon after she got home."

He measured me with his gaze. "How old are you now, Darcy?"

"I'll be fifteen in July."

He shook his head. "Where does the time go? Seems like only yesterday your mother was bringing you into my office for your baby shots."

"I've grown up," I announced.

"So you have. I hear good things about you, Darcy. I hear you're very smart and planning on going off to college in a few years."

"Only if Mama's well," I said.

He opened his medical bag and extracted a vial of clear liquid and a syringe. "You scared of needles?" he asked in his soft country drawl. "I ask because some people are."

"I'm not scared."

"I've spoken to your father," he said, "and told

him that I would like to leave a filled syringe here at the house."

"Why?"

"So that if your mother is in great pain when I'm called and I'm away from my office, I won't have to waste time stopping by my clinic to pick up supplies. I can just come straight over and give her the necessary injection."

It made sense to me. "All right," I said. All the while he was talking, he was preparing the syringe. I watched him swipe an alcohol swab across the rubber stopper on the vial, shoot air into the bottle and draw the clear liquid into the syringe. He held the filled syringe up to the light. "I'm checking for air bubbles," he explained. "You've got to thump them out or it'll affect the amount of the dose." He tapped the side of the syringe barrel with his thumb and forefinger, then held it up to the light again. "See? Clean and ready to go."

I remembered the time I'd stepped on a rusty nail and had to have a tetanus shot. "Is it hard to stick somebody?"

"Not at all," he said. "The upper buttocks and the back side of the arm are perfect sites because that's where body fat is concentrated, so it hurts less."

He snapped the protective cap over the needle and held it out to me. I took it, rolled it gently between my fingers. The needle looked long and sharp through the transparent shield. "And now it's ready?" I asked.

"Ready for injecting. Store it in a plastic food container in the back of your refrigerator, all right?"

I rummaged in the cupboard until I found a container that was the correct size to hold the syringe. Dr. Keller placed the filled syringe inside, closed the lid and gave it to me. I put it in the refrigerator.

"What's the name of the pain medicine?" I asked.

"Morphine," he said.

"And it's really strong?" I didn't want my mother to have any pain.

"Very strong," he said. He picked up his medical bag and left.

I crept into Mama's room. She was sound asleep. I didn't want to leave her, so I stretched out on the floor beneath the bay window, spread out my books and started on my homework. Papa found me there when he came home. We went downstairs, where I explained what had happened.

His expression clouded. "I had hoped she wouldn't have hurt so much, so soon."

"Me too," I said.

He sighed. "Well, I'm glad you were with her, anyway."

I told Becky about it later on the phone and she was very sympathetic. The discussion we were having on the way home was forgotten, which suited me just fine. I was tired of lying, tired of covering up. I wished I had the courage to confess all to her, but I didn't. I couldn't tell her how I felt about Jason. Not when I knew my feelings would never be returned.

Mama had good days. One afternoon, when I arrived home from school, I found her sitting on a chaise lounge in our backyard, Grandmother's quilt tucked around her. "Come sit with me, Darcy," she said.

I pulled up a lawn chair. "You feeling better?" I asked.

"Somewhat. Truth is, I just couldn't stay cooped up in that room one more minute. I had to come watch the flowers growing."

The spring day was warm and bees were busy around the heads of flowers coaxed from the ground by the sun. Overhead trees were ripe with fresh green leaves. Spent blossoms littered the ground, making a carpet of small, soft petals. I breathed in the air, washed clean by an earlier rain shower. "I thought I'd put in the begonias on Saturday," I told Mama.

"Might be best to wait another few weeks.

Sometimes March can fool you into thinking winter has gone, when it hasn't."

Daylily stalks were coming up along the edge of the beds I'd planted with pansies in the fall. The lilies were bulbs that lay dormant underground but came up every year. The white flowers generally appeared around Easter. "To remind us of the Resurrection," Mama always told me. I saw sweet flag and water mint and marsh marigolds beginning to bloom around the pond. By summer the rushes would be tall enough to whisper in the breeze.

Mama plucked at the quilt on her lap. "My garden club wants to come and take care of our gardens this spring and summer."

"Why are they trying to take over your gardens? They have gardens of their own to care for." I was irritated because it seemed to me that they were being pushy.

"I told them thank you, but that I've already asked Joe Moses to take over their care."

"I can keep up the gardens," I said, sitting up straighter.

"You have school. That's the most important thing for you."

"School will be out first of June."

"And you don't need to spend your summer slaving over this yard."

"But I *like* doing it. And I'm good at it."

"Yes, you are, but I'm just trying to make it easier for you." Her expression turned wistful. "You can't count on me helping at all, sugar. Not this year."

"I can do it by myself," I mumbled. "I really can."

She reached over and squeezed my hand. "It's all right to let go of some things—even the things we love. Sometimes, it's even best."

Her comments left me sad, and I remembered how we used to talk every day after school, but now, no more.

"Goodness, you look as sad as a one-eyed squirrel." Mama took my hand. "Must be more on your mind than the gardens. Tell me what's going on with you."

I thought about my lying for Jason. I thought about the knife and how bad things could have gotten if he'd hurt J.T. or Frankie. I thought about the wild and unsettling emotions I felt whenever I was around Jason. Yet, for some reason, I couldn't tell her any of that. Over the past months, my life had veered from the track of my parents' well-ordered world, where their rules set the standards. I had taken steps that veered away from the comfort and predictability of what was expected of me, and I'd wandered afield, making my own way down a road barely discernible but strangely exciting. "Not too much to tell, Mama," I finally said. "I'm working hard and staying out of trouble."

She must have believed me because she said, "You're a good girl, Darcy, and smart to boot. I'm so proud of you."

We sat awhile, looking out across the beds of showy flowers. "Do you still believe that angels live in gardens, Mama?" I asked, wanting to turn time back. I wanted to be little again, when Mama was well and strong.

Mama laughed and kissed my cheek. "Why, child, I hear the rush of their wings every time I come out here. Listen."

I tried, but the magic was gone. The angels had left us, alone and adrift in a world where I was afraid.

We were interrupted by Papa. He came down the back porch steps, his suit jacket thrown over his shoulders. "There you two are," he said. "I thought you'd both run away."

"I wouldn't get far," Mama said with a smile. She reached for his hand.

He bent and kissed her cheek. "May I join you?" He dragged over another lawn chair.

"Carole's bringing over supper," I told him. "Country-fried steak and mashed potatoes."

"She's very kind," Mama said.

"And a good cook," Papa added.

"Which is why you married me in the first place," Mama said.

"I married you because you bullied me into matrimony." Papa looked at me and winked.

"Bullied you?" Mama jabbed him in the ribs. "How so?"

Papa looked again at me. "She told me she was going to run off with Billy Sparks. Scared me witless. I fell to my knees right then and there and begged her to marry me."

"Would you have married Billy Sparks?" I recalled the short, plump man who owned the hardware store and made a face.

"It was only a scare tactic," Mama said.

"One that worked," Papa added. "And one that made me the happiest man alive."

Their fingers were interwined and they were staring at each other, making me feel like an intruder. I scraped back my chair and stood. "I have homework," I announced.

They didn't seem to notice when I clattered up the porch steps and slammed the screen door, leaving them to remember a past long before my time.

I confided to Becky Sue that Mama's bad days were outweighing her good ones. I didn't go to Becky's house as much as I once had—maybe on the weekends, when Papa was at home. Nor did Becky often come to my house. It wasn't anything we really discussed, it just started happening.

When I arrived home from school, the first thing I would do was check on my mother. Some days I found her sitting on the patio in the lounge chair reading her worn white leather Bible. I didn't disturb her then because she was praying and visiting with God.

But usually she was in bed, often asleep, for she took many medications. She kept the TV set turned on in her and Papa's room, "for the company," she told me. "For the sound of other voices with something else to talk about besides myself."

If she wanted anything, I brought it to her. I stayed if she let me, but she usually said, "Go on, honey. You don't have to sit in this stuffy room with me."

So I'd go downstairs to the kitchen table and start my homework. Just before six o'clock and Papa's arrival, I'd rummage through the refrigerator and begin heating up whatever was there—Papa had told Carole that the church ladies didn't have to bring supper every night, that we could make do with fewer deliveries. Although friends meant well, it was hard having them always popping over and giving us pitying looks and asking questions we couldn't answer.

We took supper upstairs and ate in the bedroom, although Mama never ate much. The pills upset her stomach and she didn't have much of an appetite.

I was doing my homework one afternoon when I heard a horrific crash from upstairs. I leaped up, took the stairs two at a time, my heart racing like a runaway train. I hurtled into Mama's room. She was sitting on the floor, her arms wrapped tightly around her, rocking to and fro and crying. Scattered on the floor were hundreds of pills and several empty brown plastic prescription bottles. The top of her dresser had been swept clean and I knew without asking that she'd done it herself. I dropped to my knees in front of her. "Mama! What's wrong?"

She wiped her eyes with her hands. "I had a fit, Darcy. An old-fashioned hissy fit." Her voice was thick with tears. "I am so tired of all these pills. I am so tired of hurting. I am so tired. . . ." Her voice trailed off and my heart contracted.

"Let me help you back to bed," I said.

She accepted my aid and I led her to the bed. I fluffed the pillows and smoothed the sheets and tucked her in.

She looked up at me, her eyes huge in her thin face. "I feel ashamed," she whispered.

"It's all right. You just rest. Can I get you some water?"

"Yes, and a pain pill too."

"Which ones are they?" I stared in dismay at the littered floor.

"They're here on my bedside table."

I fished one out and got her a glass of fresh water and she took the pill. "I—I'm sorry, Darcy, about the mess."

"Don't think anything of it," I said. "I've had a hissy fit on occasion myself."

I watched her eyelids grow heavy, and when I was certain she was asleep, I got down on my hands and knees and started picking up pills and overturned bottles, searching under the bed and the furniture and in every nook and cranny where they might have rolled. I collected every one in a basket. I lugged it downstairs and spread everything out on the kitchen table, where I sorted the pills by color, size and shape. When I was finished, I stared at the row of bottles and their medical names. I realized that I had no earthly idea what pills went in which bottle. I began to cry. That was how Papa found me when he arrived home from work—standing at the kitchen table, crying, all the pills in separate heaps, the bottles lined up like soldiers.

"What happened?" he asked.

I told him. He took me in his arms.

"I—I can't put the pills away," I said. "If I don't get them in the right bottles, Mama can't take them on time. She has to take them, Papa, or she'll die and it will be my fault."

"It's okay, baby girl. I'll call Doc Keller and he'll come over and sort things out. It's not your fault, honey. I believe that your mama's just powerful tired of being sick."

I sniffed hard. "She should be better by now, Papa . . . don't you think so?"

He did not answer but kissed my forehead and went to the phone and called the doctor.

On March 30, Easter Sunday, Da Nang, South Vietnam's second largest city, fell to the North Vietnamese Army. On April 5, Adel called from Germany, sobbing. "The army's sent Barry off on an intelligence-gathering mission. I'm all alone, Papa. I—I can't stand it one more minute here without him. I want to come home, Papa. Please say I can come home."

# Twenty-one
*April*

"I really don't like living overseas on an army base," Adel told us. "Barry was going to take me to Paris in June, but then his orders came and he was gone. I couldn't bear staying in Germany one more day without him."

Papa had picked her up at the Atlanta airport and brought her home within days of her telephone call. She said that the flight had taken "forever" and that she was nauseated, so she slept almost round the clock. Now we were sitting at the dining table after supper. Even Mama had come downstairs to join us. I had not seen Adel in three months, and I'd expected more of a change in her appearance with her pregnancy, but I detected only the slightest swelling in her abdomen.

"Well, you're home now and a sight for sore eyes," Mama said.

"Do you know how long Barry will be gone?" Papa asked.

"He doesn't know. He can't even say exactly where he is other than 'Southeast Asia' because it's an intelligence mission. I send my letters to him to a post office box in Washington, D.C., in care of the army, and they forward his mail to him. He was glad I was coming home. He wants me to be with my family."

"Do you think you can stay until the baby comes?" Papa asked.

"Depends on the army. If Barry gets reassigned someplace where I can join him, then I'll go. But if that happens, then I swear just as soon as the baby's born and I can travel, I'll come here."

"Well, I am so happy you're here right now. I can't think of anything I'd rather have than my family surrounding me." Mama's smile lit up her face, making me realize just how much she'd missed Adel. More than I had missed her, I thought, then felt uncharitable. Adel had a way of absorbing attention like a sponge soaking up water, but so long as Mama was happy, then I would be happy too.

By the end of the week after Adel's return, I had to admit that it was good that she'd come home. For starters, Mama wasn't alone all day. When I came in from school, Adel was there to greet me. Plus, she always cooked supper, a skill that she'd improved mightily since being married. Dr. Keller took over as Adel's prenatal doctor. He said that it brought him "full circle." He had delivered Adel, and if he delivered her baby, then he could retire knowing that another generation had been set in place by his hands. I knew he came to give Mama pain shots, but this was generally while I was at school and Adel was with her. I hated seeing her in pain.

At school, J.T. ignored me, which pleased me greatly, but then Jason didn't have much use for me either. If I saw him in the halls, he greeted me, but he didn't go out of his way for me. So I was surprised when I looked up from my work in the backyard on a Saturday and saw him heading toward me. The day was bright and beautiful with sunshine, and it lit up his hair with golden highlights. I asked, "And to what do I owe this visit?" Once again, I did not look my best, but at least I hadn't been working for hours, so I wasn't perspiring like a dog.

"I brought your mother something from Carole. Your sister said you were out here digging in the dirt. Thought I'd check on you."

"I enjoy gardening. Makes me feel good to help things grow." I sounded defensive even as I took off the heavy gardening gloves and flexed my fingers.

He looked around at the blooming plants. "Pretty stuff," he said, nodding toward the gazebo. Long, delicate clusters of lavender-colored wisteria flowers hung from vines growing on the railings and from the overhead trees.

"I can't take credit for their beauty, only their location," I said. "Mama and I planted those vines when I was about five. They bloom every year."

He began to stroll around the yard and I followed, although I hated myself for doing so, because I wanted to be near him for as long as possible. He stopped at every bed in bloom. "What's here?" he asked, gesturing.

"Purple rock cress, violets, Jacob's ladder, columbine," I said, using the common names of the flowers I'd watched regrow every spring of my life.

He moved to another bed where nothing was yet growing. "And here?"

"This is a bed that's 'becoming,' " I explained. "I've sown seeds and the flowers will be out later in the summer. Some will grow just because they grew here last year."

"And what will the names of these 'becoming' flowers be?" He looked amused.

I couldn't believe he was truly interested, but I told him anyway. "Snapdragons, baby's breath, foxglove, forget-me-nots, love-in-a-mist."

"Love-in-a-mist? That's a funny name." His

smile spread into his eyes and I couldn't tell if he was laughing at me. *"Nigella,"* I said coolly, using the Latin name. "Like that word better?"

"No. I like the unusual names better. What are some others?"

I knew plenty about the yard and began to feel more comfortable as we walked, for I was in my element. I pointed out the different beds and described what would eventually appear by full summer. By the time we'd made it to the far back corner, I was gushing out flower types and colors and spewing out their histories. "Now, this is one of my very, very favorites," I told him. We were standing in front of an old iron gate propped against the wooden fence at the back of our property.

"A gate to nowhere?" Jason asked, giving me a curious look.

"It's just decoration. Mama put this here after Grandmother died as a kind of living memorial. We planted it with morning-glory vines that grow up all over it and make it so pretty. I'm planning on putting in *Polygonum orientale* this year," I said, using the formal name of a plant he could not possibly know.

"English, please."

I smiled smugly. "It's called kiss-me-over-the-garden-gate. They grow tall, up to six feet, and have the prettiest little pink flowers that droop in clusters. And besides, I think it's really clever. You know, an iron garden gate with a flower named garden gate—get it?"

He grinned. "What did you call it?"

"Kiss-me-over-the-garden-gate."

And suddenly, quickly, he kissed me full on the mouth.

I was so shocked, I about fell over. "What was that for?"

"I thought you'd given me an invitation." His eyes sparkled with mischief.

I felt color creeping up my cheeks.

"Now, don't tell me no one's ever kissed you by the garden gate before."

I stared at him. "You're making fun of me."

A look of confusion crossed his face, then another expression that reminded me of the look a person gets when catching on to something for the first time. He said, "No . . . I'm not."

"You caught me by surprise," I said defensively, for I didn't want him to know how inexperienced I was. Thinking fast, I said, "A girl usually likes to be asked first. Otherwise, no telling how many fools will take to kissing her." The longer he stood looking at me, the more hotly my cheeks burned. I wanted to run away, but my feet felt rooted to the ground.

"Fair enough." Jason clasped his hands behind his back and leaned very close. "May I kiss you, Darcy?"

I knew that if I told him no, he wouldn't. And in that moment, a feeling of undeniable feminine power came over me. I could make him do whatever I wanted. Except that I *did* want him to kiss me. More than anything. "Yes," I said crisply. "You may."

He raised my chin and gently, tenderly placed his lips on mine. As if they had a mind of their own, my arms lifted to wind around his neck. His arms slipped around me, hugged me tightly. The kiss deepened and I felt like a flower opening up after rain. I pressed myself against his body. My blood sizzled and I heard a pounding in my ears that blotted out the rest of the world. The universe consisted of Jason's mouth on mine and my body trembling and wanting more. Forever hardly seemed enough time to relish the feelings pouring through me.

Abruptly, he broke off, his breathing ragged. The air between us felt charged. He pressed his forehead to mine and whispered, "Wow."

I couldn't find my voice. My knees could barely support me. "Wow" hardly expressed what I was feeling.

He let go of me, stepped away. "You'd better go back to your house."

I didn't want to go back to the house. I wanted to throw myself into Jason's arms and have him kiss me ten more times . . . a hundred more. I had never felt so wonderful as how I'd felt while he was holding me, kissing me. And now he was sending me off? Had I done something wrong? Disappointed him? Could he tell I was an amateur?

"I have garden work to finish," I said quietly, not wanting him to know how much I wanted to kiss him again. My sense of feminine power had evaporated like a drop of water on a hot skillet.

He reached out as if to touch me, quickly changed his mind, turned and jogged toward the house, leaving me alone to wonder about what I'd done to make him go away.

This kissing of Jason was not something I could keep from Becky Sue. No, not this world-shaking event. That afternoon I invited myself to her house, and when we were alone in her room, I dropped my bomb. I said, "Jason kissed me."

Her eyes went round as saucers. "Really? When? Where? Tell me about it!"

I told her the good parts, not the parts where I'd been mooning over him for months, or how he'd all but run away when he was finished kissing me. I set out my story plain and simple. He came for a visit. We walked around the yard discussing flowers. We stood in the far back, out of sight of the house, and the next thing I knew we were kissing. End of story.

"And you liked it?" Becky asked.

I grinned. "I liked it a lot."

"Didn't I tell you so?"

She didn't sound nearly as smug as I thought she would. After all, I'd dismissed her notions of heart-thumping romance for years, and now I was saying such a thing was possible. "It doesn't pain me one bit to admit you were absolutely correct."

She flopped back on her bed dramatically. "By the way, I hate you."

"But why?"

She bounced up. "Because I was going to tell you that Russell had kissed me and that it was awful."

"How awful?"

"He kisses like a fish—wet and sloppy." She sucked in her cheeks and moved her lips like a guppy in a fishbowl.

I started laughing.

"I was pinning all my hopes on Russell, and come to find out he kisses so poorly that I don't ever want him to kiss me again. If I wanted to get licked, I'd get me a dog!" She made a face. "Are you laughing at me?"

"Wouldn't think of it," I told her between giggles.

She bopped me with a bed pillow, and the next thing I knew we were rolling on the bed, squealing and popping each other with pillows.

When we stopped to catch our breath, she leaned close to my face. "So tell me about kissing Jason. What was it like? And don't you leave out one detail!"

I thought of how best to describe it. "It was like being on fire, but not getting burned up. It was like floating on water and feeling soft as velvet on my insides. It was like being free and flying . . . and . . . and it was . . . wonderful!" I ran out of words.

"Lucky you," Becky said wistfully. "Is he your boyfriend now?"

She stopped me cold with that one and my good humor evaporated. I rolled so that my back was to her and she couldn't see the pain I was feeling in my heart. "Course not. It was just a kiss, Becky Sue. It was just for fun. And it didn't really mean a thing. Not to either of us."

# Twenty-two

Now that Barry was somewhere in Southeast Asia, Adel and I followed the news from that area on television and in the newspapers religiously. In Vietnam, the North Vietnamese Army had become an unstoppable juggernaut. In Cambodia, adjacent to Vietnam, the Khmer Rouge captured the capital city of Phnom Penh, and stories of terrible atrocities were being reported. "I sure hope the army didn't send him there," Adel would say after the evening news, concern etched in her pretty face.

Here at home, our nation was weary of the war and eager to be free of it and the black mark it had left on our reputation as defenders of democracy. At least that was what the editorials in the papers were saying. It just made Adel angry because she saw the war from a different perspective, that of a soldier's wife, where the war was justifiable. I couldn't blame her. As I wrote my report to go with my chart, I wondered, *Why have so many died for a cause that has lost its virtue?*

In the waning days of April, it was also becoming obvious that my mother was losing her personal war with cancer. We never said it aloud to one another, but nevertheless, it was true, even to my eyes. The rows of pill bottles went largely untouched as she stopped taking the medications that left her too weak to stand, too sick to care. Managing the pain of her bone cancer became our family's focus. There were no more "good and bad days." Only bad ones. Coming home from school and seeing Dr. Keller's car in our driveway was commonplace for me.

Then one day I came home to Adel crying in the kitchen and near hysterics. I dropped my books and they scattered across the floor. Fear knotted like a vise around my heart. "What happened? Mama didn't—Mama isn't—" I couldn't get the word out.

Adel kept twisting her hands together. "No, no," she cried, for she knew what I was asking. "She's just in terrible pain, and Dr. Keller can't come."

"What do you mean he can't come?"

"There was an accident. One of the farmworkers got caught in a combine and Doc's working hard to save the man's arm. His nurse says he'll come as soon as he can, but Mama needs him now!"

I took the stairs two at a time and rushed into Mama's room. She lay on the bed, moaning, begging for help. Her skin was pale as white chalk. I dropped at the side of the bed, took her hand. "Mama? It's Darcy. Would you like a cold cloth?"

She didn't answer. She couldn't. Pain racked her body and she writhed on the bed. The sheets were twisted and soaked with sweat and vomit.

Adel appeared next to me. I jumped up and grabbed her by the shoulders. Fury consumed me. How could she have allowed our mother to lie there in filth? "What have you done for her? What about her pain pills?"

"She can't keep anything down." Adel's eyes were wild with fear. "Don't you think I've been trying? She throws everything up as soon as it hits her stomach. I even crushed a pill in water, but she couldn't keep it down either."

My brain went numb. How could this be happening? "Call the doctor again."

"I just hung up. He can't come now, Darcy. He'll come as soon as he can."

"But Mama needs him now!"

"He can't come now, Darcy!"

We were shouting at each other.

"Papa—" I said.

"You know he's out of town."

I had forgotten that Papa was at a one-day banking seminar in Atlanta. There was nothing he could have done for Mama anyway.

Mama moaned, cried out to Jesus to help her, began heaving. Adel grabbed a bowl, knelt beside the bed and held the bowl under Mama's mouth. "It's okay, Mama. We're right here, Mama. We won't leave you, Mama." She used a soothing voice as one might talk to a child.

"Let me die! Let me die!" Mama sobbed.

In that instant, I knew what had to be done. I said to Adel, "I can help her. Wait. I'll be right back."

I ran down the hall, bolted down the stairs. In the kitchen, I jerked open the refrigerator door and starting tossing aside cans and containers, all the while pleading, "Let it be here. Please let it be here." I dragged out the container that held the syringe full of morphine and ran back upstairs.

Adel's eyes widened as I advanced to the bed, the needle in my hand. "What are you doing?" She grabbed my arm.

"I'm helping Mama. Doc Keller made this up and left it here. He showed me how to use it." I had fudged on the truth of the second part, but desperation had made me brave. I saw instantly that Adel believed me because she wanted to believe me.

"All right," she said, standing aside. "What can I do?"

I said a quick prayer, because if anyone needed help from God at that moment, it was me. "Just hold her steady. I don't want to hurt her."

Mama sobbed and whimpered. Adel took our mother's arm and I bathed the skin with a splash of rubbing alcohol. The sharp odor stung the air. *In the fatty tissue,* Dr. Keller had explained. Mama looked to be skin and bones, but I pinched up her skin, aimed the tip of the needle toward the back of the arm, where the flesh appeared to be the meatiest. The needle sank quickly. I pushed the plunger steadily, but not too fast, while Adel restrained Mama and talked to her. In amazement, I saw that although my heart was racing and my breathing was shallow, my hands were steady as a rock.

Once the syringe was empty, I extracted the needle and capped it. Adel cradled Mama, rocked her back and forth. Mama's moaning and wild thrashing slowed as the morphine did its job. When she was at rest, Adel laid her back onto the pillow and wiped her face with a damp washcloth.

Adel and I looked into each other's eyes, measuring, evaluating, as if seeing one another in a whole new light. Finally Adel said, "She'll sleep now."

"Yes," I said. My legs felt wobbly and I rested my hand on the wall for support.

"I'm going to change her sheets. I know how to do it with her in the bed. Why don't you go sit on the porch and wait for Dr. Keller?"

I did. I sat on the porch steps, letting the warm sun soak the coldness out of me. My heart had stopped pounding, but my cheeks were wet with tears. How much suffering could one person take?

I didn't know how much time passed, but eventually Dr. Keller's car swung into our driveway. I met him on the lawn and told him what I'd done. He nodded, went inside and up the stairs. I waited in the hallway. When he came out, he said, "Your mother's resting peacefully."

My tongue felt thick with emotion.

He patted my shoulder. "You did well, Darcy."

"I—I was so scared."

"We all get scared."

"That's why you showed me about the morphine and syringe, isn't it? So I could give Mama a shot if I had to."

He simply squeezed my shoulder and started toward the kitchen. "I'm making up another injection." He paused, turned to look at me. "This was a fluke, Darcy, my being tied up like I was. It should never happen again."

I cleared my throat. "How's the man who had the accident?"

"Saved his arm. And that's a good thing."

Mama awoke much later that evening. Adel and I were cleaning her room, Adel rubbing down the rugs and furniture with Pine Sol, me following behind with lemon polish. The aromas fought each other for survival.

"Hey," Mama said, her voice husky. "Have I been sleeping for long?"

We dropped what we were doing and went to her bedside. "Just a few hours. How are you feeling?" Adel asked.

"Numb."

"I fixed some soup," Adel said. "Let me bring you a bowl."

"In a minute. Sit here with me. Both of you."

We climbed into the bed, one on either side of her.

"Is your papa home?"

"Not yet."

"I don't even remember Dr. Keller coming."

Adel and I exchanged glances, and immediately we both knew we weren't going to tell her about how I'd given her the shot. "You were hurting pretty bad," I told her. "But Doc Keller took care of you."

She closed her eyes, licked her lips. "He's a good man."

All of a sudden, Adel took a quick breath and sat up straight, her hands cupping her abdomen. "I think I feel the baby moving!" She sat perfectly still. "It's a fluttering sensation. Like . . . a tickle."

"Let me feel."

Mama and I both put our hands on Adel's swollen abdomen. "I think I feel it," Mama said, a slow, lazy smile crossing her face.

I didn't feel a thing. "You sure?" I asked.

Adel said, "Wait a minute." She left the room, but returned minutes later with a stethoscope. "Dr. Keller loaned this to me." She put in the earpieces and placed the round silver disk against her lower abdomen. Her perfect mouth swept up into a smile. "I can hear its heartbeat," she told us.

"Let me listen," Mama said.

Adel put the earpieces into Mama's ears. After a minute, Mama's eyes grew misty. "Oh, yes, Adel. I hear it. Nice and strong."

Not to be left out, I said, "Me too."

I listened through the earpieces and heard a faint swoosh. "You sure that's not your dinner digesting?"

Adel gave me a playful swat. "That's your niece or nephew."

I listened again, felt a sense of wonderment. My sister had a baby growing inside her! Up until then, it hadn't seemed real to me. "What do you think it is, Mama? Boy or girl?" I asked.

"No way to tell till it's born. Course, there are some old wives' tales about predicting a baby's sex by using a string and a coin. When your father and I tried it, it pointed to us having two boys."

"Well, one out of two isn't bad," Adel said, reaching over Mama and patting my arm.

"Very funny." I smirked, but truth was, nothing could have spoiled my good mood. Snuggling next to Mama, talking about the coming baby and seeing her pain-free and happy was wonderful. The bedside lamp threw a pool of yellow light over us and I felt warm and safe.

Mama kissed me and Adel. "I wouldn't have traded two smelly old boys for my two precious girls," she said. "Not in a million years."

"Barry says he doesn't care what we have, just so long as it's healthy."

"What's it going to call you, Mama?" I asked, remembering my grandmother. She had been tall and slim with a long white braid that hung down her back. She read me bedtime stories and taught me the alphabet and how to sound out words. I always called her Grandmother because she seemed too regal for "Grandma," or even "Nana," Becky Sue's name for her grandmother.

"How about Queen Mum?" Mama said, her eyelids looking heavy.

We giggled.

"I love you two so much," Mama said.

"We love you too, Mama," Adel said, speaking for both of us. "You hungry? You want me to bring that soup?"

"In a minute," Mama said. "I just want my arms around my babies right now."

I cuddled closer. The pine disinfectant and lemon smells had lessened and all I smelled was the faintly lavender scent of my mother's skin. She leaned her head back against the headboard and closed her eyes.

It was the last time I ever saw my mother smile.

# Twenty-three

I stayed home from school during the last ten days in April. My mother was dying, and I could not leave her side. Between injections of pain medications, which Dr. Keller administered every six hours, she slept. I was told that morphine was a powerful narcotic. Adel asked if it was all right to give the shots so frequently, if Mama might not get addicted, and Dr. Keller said, "I know of doctors who think that way, but not me. I believe that pain should be managed, controlled. There's no call for a patient to be in pain if we can prevent it."

No one had to tell me that bone cancer was painful. I knew the truth whenever the morphine started wearing off and my mother cried out in agony.

Mama stopped eating, and before my eyes seemed to grow smaller in her bed, as if shrinking and drying up like a husk fixing to blow away with the next spring breeze. We moved her bed against the window, where she could look out on her gardens as she slipped in and out of consciousness. I cut flowers and arranged bouquets of pale lilies, branches of pink and white dogwood, vibrant purple irises and yellow gladiolas in vases around the room in the hope that the glorious blossoms would cheer her if she woke. Papa set up the cot on the other side of their room, where he slept, so as not to disturb her.

Friends from church and her garden club called every day. Adel took the calls usually, because I found it hard to be civil to people who called to get updates, like you would a flight that's running behind schedule. I talked with Becky Sue, but not for long spells. I had no interest in stupid school gossip. She ended up crying during our conversations anyway, and I was doing enough crying on my own.

The only people outside of family we allowed to visit Mama were Carole and Pastor Jim. Mama had asked early on for him to come and read the Psalms to her, so he came each day in the late afternoon, opened his Bible and read from the hymns of King David. I had no way of knowing if she heard him, although Dr. Keller told us that hearing was the last of the five senses to go. "I'm sure she's comforted," he'd say.

Adel had not heard from Barry, and she was worried about him. Our whole family was worried. We kept our TV sets turned on from sign-on until sign-off, just in case there were any breaking news bulletins. One by one, the cities of South Vietnam fell like dominoes as the North Vietnamese Army pressed toward Saigon, where the last bastion of America stood, the United States Embassy, with the personnel who worked there and defended it. Caring for Mama's needs kept our hands busy, but my mind was in constant turmoil. Sometimes I heard Adel crying when she thought she was alone.

On April 29, newscasters broke into the regular programming to announce the pullout of all U.S. personnel from Saigon. The Communist army was advancing swiftly and the southern government was collapsing. Vietnam is exactly twelve hours ahead of Georgia on the clock, so we started receiving pictures and news footage of the April 30 pullout. The next morning, Dr. Keller alerted us that Mama's breathing patterns had changed. My heart felt icy cold when he said it, because he looked us in the eyes and added, "The end is near."

We remained in Mama's room with her all that day—me, Adel and Papa. Dr. Keller hung around the house, told us to call him in if we needed him. When Pastor Jim arrived, Papa asked him to please read the Twenty-third Psalm, ". . . and keep reading it," because it was Mama's favorite. His soft, resonant voice offered up the words that were so familiar to us. " 'The Lord is my Shepherd; I shall not want. He maketh me to lie down in green pastures, He leadeth me beside still waters. He restoreth my soul. . . .' "

Outside, a fine spring rain was falling—rain laced through with sunlight, a rare phenomenon. On the far side of the room, the television played the evening news. The sound was muted, but the images shone in black-and-white newsreel relief. On the screen, I watched frantic people running through burning streets and throwing their bodies at the locked iron gates of the U.S. Embassy, where armed marines stood and blocked entry into the hallowed grounds.

" 'He guideth me in the paths of righteousness for his name's sake. Yea, though I walk through the valley of the shadow of death, I will fear no evil . . . ,' " Pastor Jim read.

I saw helicopters, their blades whipping up debris as they lifted off from rooftops, people clinging frantically to the open doorways, all desperate to climb aboard, to escape the coming horror of enemy takeover.

" '. . . for Thou art with me. Thy rod and Thy staff, they comfort me. . . .' "

The camera's eye blinked and the picture changed to one of tanks that rolled in advance of scores of foot soldiers. The battalions looked like ants swarming toward the perimeters of the chaotic city—ants, wild and ferocious and mad with purpose.

" 'Thou preparest a table before me in the presence of mine enemies, Thou anointest my head with oil, my cup runneth over. . . .' "

In the room where my mother lay, another enemy, as old as time, was approaching. We were powerless, defenseless, and could not stop it. We held on to Mama's hands in an effort to link her with our world of the living. Mama's labored breathing sounded like tearing paper, the ragged edges fluttering and tattered beyond repair. The rhythm of her breath was ever changing—long, then short . . . fast, then slow. I watched her chest move up and down. The breathing had become hard work for her. So hard. Too hard.

" '. . . Surely goodness and mercy shall follow me, all the days of my life. . . .' "

On the TV screen, another empty chopper set down on embassy soil and people scrambled into the open cavern of its side. It filled quickly and soldiers crossed their bayonets over the doorway to stop the piling on of more people. Hands reached upward in desperate supplication as the chopper wobbled and lifted under the weight. I saw a woman toss a bundle upward into the arms of another reaching down. The bundle wiggled and a baby emerged. The woman below held up outstretched arms, but the chopper was crammed full and it left without her. I could see that her baby was safe, but she remained behind, terror etched in her face, her mouth open, screaming.

The chopper rose, creating a windstorm that flattened those left behind. The chopper circled the embassy compound, then headed off into a cloudless sky toward freedom. I remembered Kyle's words about choppers at the siege of Khe Sanh, *the choppers rise up like great dark angels*, and then I understood that the dark angels had also come for my mother's soul. That death would be a release. That it was selfish of me to ask her to remain. I silently gave her permission to leave this place of pain and suffering. I told her she was free to go and leave her cancer-riddled body behind. The great dark angels would take her up, up into the gardens of paradise.

My vision blurred with tears. I saw her face as

through a mist. I felt her fingers loosen their grip as she let go of life and her soul spilled over into eternity, where she would dwell in the House of the Lord,

Forever.

# Twenty-four
## *May–August*

My world turned gray after my mother died. In my eyes, the gardens lost their color, and my life its focus. On the day we buried Mama, I hardly saw the crowds of people, but Adel told me that most of Conners turned out to pay their respects. I had released her to that cloud of dark angels, represented so dramatically in my mind by the rescue choppers in Vietnam on that last day in April, and so I honestly believed that the funeral was extraneous and redundant, done for the sake of the living and not the dead.

In mid-May, the church held its annual mother-daughter banquet, and Carole said she'd be proud to escort me and Adel to an event neither of us had ever missed. My sister and I had better sense and saved ourselves terrible pain. We said thank you for the offer, and we stayed home.

Adel finally heard from Barry, but his letters left her unsatisfied. He said nothing about his duties ending or if he was in harm's way. He told her about the weather and a few stories about bad food, and of how much he missed her, but no real information. Her letters took time getting to him, because he didn't know about Mama's death until almost the end of May, and by the time his heartfelt sorrow returned to Adel, it was the middle of June.

As Adel's pregnancy advanced, we pored over baby books together just so we could get a picture in our minds of what it might look like at four, five and six months. She let me feel it move and I teased her with, "Goodness, I think it's going to kick its way out."

"I hope Barry can be with me when it comes," she often told me. "I don't want to have this baby all alone."

Eventually, the school year ended. I passed with high grades, despite my absences. Mr. Kessler gave me an A+ on my war chart project for government class, but I knew it was Barry's loan of Kyle's war journal that put me over the top. Before turning it in, I wrote in the final American casualty count for Vietnam—58, 195, the last two deaths happening on April 30, 1975. I also added, "Over 150,000 were seriously wounded, and a thousand are still missing in action."

In June right after school ended, Jason came to the house to see me. I had not been alone with him since the day he had kissed me. And although so much had happened in my life since then, I had not forgotten one moment of it. I was happy to see him, pleased that he'd made a special trip. He asked to go out into the yard, and once we were sitting on the bench overlooking the pond, he said, "I'm sorry about your mother."

"Thank you," I said, still feeling the sting of her death each time it was mentioned. He looked as if something else was on his mind, so I asked, "Is there anything else?"

"I've come to tell you goodbye."

He had my full attention. "Where are you going?"

"Home . . . back to Chicago."

I kept my eyes on the pond. I wasn't sure I could look him in the face without him knowing how much his words had rocked me. "What's Carole think?"

"She's not in favor of it, but I'm eighteen now and I can do what I want."

"You had a birthday?"

"May thirtieth," he said. "I finished school, like I promised, so now there's no reason for me to stay here."

I looked at him then, because his words stung

me. "You're not going to go through the graduation ceremony?"

"The school can mail me my diploma."

"Don't you think Carole would like to see you
walk?"

He shrugged. "Doesn't matter. I'm going. I'm
riding my cycle back."

"It's a long way to Chicago," I said, surprised
by such an idea. "What about your stuff . . . you
know, personal things?"

"Carole and Jim will ship what I can't fit on
the back of the machine."

The surface of the pond was disturbed by an
insect, and I watched the water travel in concen-
tric circles before hitting the rushes. The circles
spread out in ripples that didn't touch and I realized that that was what would become of my rela-
tionship with Jason. Once he left, we wouldn't
touch again.

"I guess this is really goodbye then," I said,
feeling weepy. I quashed the desire to cry.

"It is." He stood, moved in front of me, but I
stayed seated on the bench. "Don't let Rucker
hassle you next year."

I shrugged. "He seems to have lost interest in
giving me a hard time. I guess even J.T. loses interest." I said what I did because that was the way
I felt toward Jason—he'd lost interest in me. And

why shouldn't he? I was years younger and pretty boring for a boy like him.

"You're the only one I'm telling goodbye personally," he added.

"Is that supposed to make me special?"

"You are special."

I glanced up to make certain he wasn't patronizing me. "I don't feel special."

He took my hands into his and pulled me up so that we were facing each other. Heat from the summer day had made his hair damp, and long strands of it lay across his forehead. I wanted so much to reach up and touch it. I didn't. He said, "I never told you this before, but I promised Carole two things last fall. I told her I'd finish school. And I told her I wouldn't put any moves on you."

"But why would you promise her that?"

"Because she asked me to stay clear of you. She said, 'Darcy Quinlin is off-limits.' She told me that I wasn't to hustle you or date you or go after you in any way."

"Why?" I could hardly believe what he was telling me.

"She said that your family means the world to her and she didn't want me doing anything that might hurt you or upset your parents. I fudged on my promise to her that afternoon in your garden. That's why I left so fast. I wanted a whole lot more, Darcy, but I knew I had to keep my promise."

"B-but why would she even ask such a thing from you? It doesn't make sense." I was growing angry because Carole had meddled and she'd had no right to do that.

Jason grinned, lifted my chin with his fore-finger. "It makes perfect sense. I told you once that I wasn't a nice guy. That's the truth. And you're a nice girl. And that's the truth."

"So I'm too nice to mess around with?" I was getting angrier.

He studied my face, then said, "Why would you let any guy 'mess around' with you? You're worth more than that."

His question caught me off guard and I felt my cheeks growing warmer. "I—I didn't mean—"

"I know what you meant," he said. "But hear this. If we had started something, I couldn't have stopped. I wouldn't have wanted to stop. You know what I'm saying?"

Of course I did. And the thought of it made my face hot, and I knew I was blushing full-tilt. Without pausing to think about it, I threw my arms around his neck and kissed him hard. His arms swept around me and pressed me closer. All the emotions that had held me captive for the past months—grief, longing, frustration, anger, fear—boiled up inside me. An explosion of desire shot through my body like a flash fire. I felt his hands moving on me, and everywhere he touched begged for more.

Just as suddenly, I pushed him away. I took in great gulps of air. "Goodbye!" I cried. I ran for the house like a panicked rabbit. I ran because if I'd stayed, no promise in the world would have protected either of us from what would have happened next.

My mother always said that bad things happen in threes. For me, I counted the death of my mother, followed by the loss of Jason, as two. I waited expectantly for the third. It came in late August, when the army notified Adel that, "while on a routine mission," Barry had stepped on a land mine and blown off his left leg.

# Twenty-five
## *November*

᚛ ᚛

Adel was seven months pregnant in August, when Papa and I said goodbye to her at the Atlanta airport. She was set to fly back to Germany and the army hospital where Barry had been sent to heal.

"You take care of yourself, little lady," Papa said, kissing her tear-streaked cheek. "I can't stand much more sadness. You hear?"

"I'll take care, Papa," she said.

I hugged her hard. "Tell Barry to get well quick."

We watched her fly away, feeling the loss of both Adel and the tiny person she carried inside her, beneath her heart.

Adel called from Germany to tell us that Barry was doing well enough, and that he'd been overjoyed to see her. He had been on a mission in

Cambodia, where land mines were sprinkled in the ground like bits of pepper. With one misstep, Barry had lost his leg and ended his career with the army.

After that, Adel called weekly with updates of Barry's progress. In the following months he advanced from a wheelchair to crutches and finally to a prosthetic leg and learned to walk all over again. He was released from the hospital and rehab, and two days later, Adel, almost twelve days overdue, went into labor.

On November 11, 1975, Veterans Day, Joy Rebecca Quinlin Sorenson came into this world, weighing eight pounds and seven ounces, and with a full head of soft black hair. "She's beautiful!" Barry said in the phone call he made to us.

"You named her after Mama and *me?*" I asked, hardly believing what he had told me.

"Adel says the names sound good together and that she hoped you wouldn't mind."

"I don't mind. I love it!"

"When will you get your discharge papers?" Papa asked.

Barry answered, "We'll be there for Thanksgiving."

They arrived two days before the holiday. My new niece was a wonder with a rosebud mouth and a plump little face. Barry looked thinner, but just as handsome. I couldn't tell that his left leg was not flesh and blood until he pulled up his pant leg and showed me the beige plastic, jointed by metal links at the knee.

"Looks real," I said.

"No it doesn't," he said. "I have phantom pains sometimes that make me *think* it's my real leg, but it isn't. I'm just glad to be alive."

Being a sophomore in good standing, I didn't bother going to school on Wednesday. How could I sit in a classroom when Adel, Barry and the baby were at the house? Becky Sue dropped over to see the baby. She carried on about how pretty she was, then went on her way, for she had a new boyfriend and he was taking her over to meet his visiting grandparents.

Adel and I whipped up a turkey and all the trimmings and our family sat down together on Thanksgiving Day to celebrate. I couldn't keep my eyes off my mother's empty chair. Had it only been a year since she'd first come home from the hospital? Since Adel and Barry got engaged? As Papa asked the blessing, I felt sorrow rise to my throat, longing for her in my heart.

When I looked up, I saw Adel wiping her eyes with her napkin.

Later, when we were sitting in the living room and Joy Rebecca was sleeping, I gave Adel the special gift I'd made for my niece. "It's a scrapbook," I said, setting the large album on her lap. "I got the idea from the one Kyle made about the war. This one's happy."

I'd filled the pages with photos of our family. Of Mama and Papa on their wedding day, of Adel as a baby, of Adel's school pictures, of me with Adel. "I thought she'd like to see that her mother was a princess," I said when we came to the pages where Adel wore various pageant and home-coming crowns. "I left pages blank for you, Barry," I explained. "For your baby pictures and growing-up pictures."

In the middle of the book, I'd drawn a family tree and written in all the names I knew, all the way back as far as I'd ever heard Mama say. Papa had helped me label his branches, and again, I'd left Barry's branches bare for him to fill in.

By now Adel was weeping and, for the first time in my memory, speechless. Then the baby started crying and Adel hurried from the room to nurse her. Barry smoothed his hand over the cover of the book. "You do nice work, Darcy. Thank you. We'll treasure it always."

I went upstairs and into Adel and Barry's room, where my sister was sitting in the old rocker Papa had dragged down from the attic. "The same one where your mother nursed you girls," he had told us.

I tiptoed over and watched the baby nursing. The baby sucked greedily, taking the nourishment that belonged to her by God's design. I recalled all the times I had longed for larger breasts, then the times I didn't want any because of Mama's breast cancer. What had seemed useless and frightening to me months before now seemed perfect and necessary.

"Your present is wonderful." Adel's voice was thick with unshed tears.

"I'm glad you like it."

"I sure do miss Mama. I'd give almost anything to talk to her again."

"So would I."

"You were lucky to have been able to spend the time with her you did while I was stuck in Germany, before Barry left. I was lonely and had nothing to do over there."

"But you're a mother now," I said. "You have plenty to keep you busy."

"And this exempts me from wanting *my* mother?"

"I guess not," I mumbled.

"I want to show her my baby. Why do you think I got pregnant so soon after getting married?"

Feeling guilty because I had counted the months between her marriage and the baby's due date like all the others in our town, I didn't answer.

"I knew Mama was dying. I wanted her to hold her first grandchild before she did."

I saw then that the hole in Adel's heart was as big as mine, just a different shape.

"Will we ever get over missing her?" I asked.

"She told me once that she never got over missing her mother, so no, I don't think we will."

By now, Joy Rebecca had fallen asleep. Adel shifted, tucked herself back into her clothing and held the baby up to me. "Hold her while I get her crib sheet out of the dryer and make up her bed."

I took the baby and Adel left. The room went whisper quiet. The rocker creaked. The baby's milk-sated breath touched my cheek. There was a night-light on in the room, so the darkness had no edges, just soft smudges. I gazed down at Joy Rebecca, and in the baby's tiny, perfect features, I saw my mother's vanished face. And also my grandmother's, and Great-grandmother Rebecca's. I saw Papa too, and Barry, and all the people who had come before him, although I had never met them or even known them. Each generation stamps itself into the next one. The impression is indelible. Like the flowers in my mother's gardens that come and go with the changing of the seasons, life re-creates itself. And the best of life must be nurtured if it is to thrive.

"I'm going to tell you about your grandmother," I whispered to the sleeping baby. "I'm going to tell you about all of your grandmothers because they are *in* you. They *are* you." And I also promised that one day, I would take her into her grandmother's gardens, where I would tell her the names of all the flowers . . . their Latin names, their common names, even their funny folk names, like love-in-a-mist and kiss-me-over-the-garden-gate.

I would do it because she belonged to *us*. And because families endure. No matter what.

# Epilogue

Like water over stones, years have passed since that time when I first joined the sorority of motherless daughters. I am older, hopefully wiser, a whole lot less naive, a whole lot more comfortable with who I am.

Much has changed in the world since those days in the seventies.

A stunning granite memorial has been built in Washington, D.C., for the people who gave their lives for their country while serving in Vietnam.

Women's health issues are much more in the forefront of medicine. Breast cancer is talked about openly. Funds are committed to its eradication.

Ronald McDonald Houses have been built near hospitals where families of patients can stay while their loved ones undergo long-term treatments.

Hospice has become a far-reaching support system for the dying and for their families.

Much has changed too for those I've known.

My hometown, Conners, has grown into a city. Today over fourteen thousand people call it home, and with expressways and fast cars, it's practically a suburb of Atlanta.

My niece, Joy Rebecca, has grown into a lovely young woman. She earned a master's degree in archaeology and has traveled to many exotic places, where she digs up and catalogs lives and civilizations from long ago. Mama would be so proud of her, just as I am.

J. T. Rucker, the nemesis of my youth, eventually married Donna. They had three children and divorced. Donna moved away after that. J.T. never achieved those glory days of high school football again. He resides in Conners and owns a car wash.

Papa never remarried. He lived alone in the old house until he had a stroke and Barry and Adel moved in with him. They renovated the kitchen and turned the back porch into two small bedrooms for their twin girls, born four years after Joy Rebecca. Papa died in 1989, sitting in a lawn chair looking out onto Mama's gardens. Adel found him. She said that his Bible was open on his lap to Psalm Twenty-three, and that he looked as if he had just fallen asleep. The doctor said he had had a massive coronary and probably never felt a thing.

Becky Sue married and moved away to California, where she and her family live. We connect with birthday and Christmas cards, e-mails and, occasionally, phone calls. She says she's happy, but that it took "several years of intensive therapy to get my Southern mentality to adapt to the California lifestyle." I've never known a better friend.

Carole and Jim moved on to other churches. We exchanged Christmas cards for years. The saddest arrived in 1982. Carole wrote that Jason had been killed in a motorcycle accident. His cycle skidded on a patch of ice and hit a tree, and Jason was thrown off. He died at the scene. I cried buckets—not only because he was dead, but also because he was once so much a part of my heart. He was a misfit. A rogue. Carole said that he never found his place in life. Yet I never forgot him and that warm April day when he kissed me and I caught a glimpse of myself as a woman in waiting. Mama said that a girl never forgets her first kiss. And she was right.

Adel hasn't gotten to Paris yet. She and Barry live in Conners. Barry set up a small repair shop where he fixes electronic gadgets for the locals. When computers appeared on the American scene, Barry adapted, and today he runs the most successful business in Conners. I asked him once if he thought losing his leg had shortchanged his life, and he told me, "I regret not having a career with the military. As for the leg . . . well, I was serving my country, and for that I'll always be proud."

His brother, Kyle, still suffers flashbacks of his war experiences. He has been in and out of VA hospitals for years, and all doubt that he will ever fully recover.

Adel and Barry raised three wonderful daughters. Adel keeps Mama's gardens beautifully, and every time I visit I tell her so. She's added angel statuary in every bed, some of them large and Victorian, some small and as delicate as the wings of butterflies. Ours are still the finest gardens, for their size, in all of Georgia. In another of life's ironies, Adel is president of the garden club. She knows more than anyone about growing things, how to keep and nurture them. Why, even the sulky roses thrive under her care.

A few years back, Adel had a scare when a lump was discovered in her breast during a routine mammogram. I packed a bag and flew to her side and waited through the surgery, all the while praying for the news to be good. And it was good.

The lump was only a cyst, easily drained. We rejoiced by going to Palm Beach to shop.

And much has changed for me.

I left Conners when I went off to college, and I never moved back. I graduated from medical school, married a fine man and am raising two sons. Today, my husband and I have a home in Appalachia, where I practice medicine and he writes books. I like the people in these hills, for they remind me of the ones I grew up with in Conners. And I fight fiercely for good medical care for them. My main soapbox is annual mammograms for every woman over forty-five. These breast X rays have saved the lives of thousands of women, because we have learned that when caught early and treated aggressively, breast cancer can be beaten.

When I drive alone in the mountains, I often think back to that pivotal year of my mother's illness and death from breast cancer. What a time it was! The loss of Mama, the specter of breast cancer that hovers over our family to this day, the war so far away, the pain, the happiness—all those things molded me into who I am today.

I miss my mother and all the parts of my life I never got to share with her, and I look forward to the time we'll meet again in heaven. I got over my anger at God for taking my mother when she was so young. Perhaps it's my medical practice that has mellowed me toward him, for I have seen great miracles happen. Or perhaps it is just who I am. I cannot hold a grudge.

Yet for all my medical training, I still marvel at the simplicity of the cycle of life, and of the complexity of the forces that drive it.

Love of God, country, family—this is the great triad that supports and sustains great civilizations. And it is, as my mother always said, "the Southern gospel."

I embrace no other.

# Afterword

Dear Reader,

I am both a mother and a daughter. For me, becoming a mother ignited my understanding of my own mother's choices, choices I often didn't "get" while growing up. As a mother myself, I realized that mothers want to take care of their children, protect them, help them over life's bumps. How devastating it would be to not be around to watch my kids grow up. And how devastating for a child to lose his mother prematurely and miss out on this kind of nurturing.

For many years, I have wanted to write the story of a mother dying prematurely. Yet every time I started, I quit because my writer's instincts kept telling me, "This isn't working." So I'd put the project aside and write about something else. Then two things happened that changed the way I thought about the novel.

In October 1993, I was diagnosed with breast cancer. I was fortunate in that my cancer was caught in its earliest stages by a routine mammogram. I was a good candidate for breast-saving surgery, so only the lump and some surrounding tissue were removed. My surgery was followed by six weeks of radiation. I now go for annual checkups, and I'm happy to say that so far, I'm cancer-free. The support of family, friends and good doctors helped me through this difficult period.

In September 1999, my beloved mother died. The loss I felt was enormous, more than I'd ever imagined possible. Again, family and friends were there for me. Out of these two experiences, the pain of losing my mother and the trauma of being diagnosed with cancer, the seeds of a story began to grow. I sat down and this time everything came together. I wrote the book you've just read.

By setting the story in the mid-seventies, I was able to revisit a time that I lived through and am now able to see through different, adult eyes. I was also able to see just how far we've come in the diagnosis and treatment of breast cancer. The Vietnam War is long over. The war against breast cancer continues. Medical science has a better arsenal to attack it. Twenty years ago, only six percent of tumors were *caught. Today, more than twenty percent are caught before they advance and grow. Doctors are better equipped to locate and exterminate the "enemy" with advanced chemotherapy, "smart" drugs that bind to the cancer receptors at the cellular level and potent "seeds" of radiation that target only the tumor. But women still die. Daughters still lose their mothers. Mothers still lose their daughters. Today, research predicts that one in five women will get breast cancer.*

*During the past twenty-five years, many support groups and organizations have emerged to help women deal with a diagnosis of breast cancer. There's a wealth of information that can help people and their families cope. You can visit many Web sites for more information, or call information hotlines. Some of these groups include:*

Y-ME National Breast Cancer Organization:
1-800-221-2141, www.y-me.org
Susan G. Komen Breast Cancer Foundation:
1-800-I'M AWARE, www.komen.org
American Cancer Society:
1-800-ACS-2345, www.cancer.org
National Cancer Institute:
1-800-4-CANCER, www.cancer.gov

*My hope for all of you is that breast cancer will be eradicated in your lifetime, but should this disease af-*

flict someone you know and love, I send you my heartfelt wishes for courage and strength. We are all connected by love and hope for the future.

All my best to you,

Lurlene

# About the Author

Lurlene McDaniel began writing inspirational novels about teenagers facing life-altering situations when her son was diagnosed with juvenile diabetes. "I saw firsthand how chronic illness affects every aspect of a person's life," she has said. "I want kids to know that while people don't get to choose what life gives to them, they do get to choose how they respond."

Lurlene McDaniel's novels are hard-hitting and realistic, but also leave readers with inspiration and hope. Her books have received acclaim from readers, teachers, parents and reviewers. Her novel *Angels Watching Over Me* and its companions, *Lifted Up by Angels* and *Until Angels Close My Eyes*, have all been national bestsellers, as have *Don't Die, My Love*; *I'll Be Seeing You*; and

*Till Death Do Us Part. Six Months to Live* was included in a literary time capsule at the Library of Congress in Washington, D.C.

Lurlene McDaniel lives in Chattanooga, Tennessee.